D1483235

*Between Father
and Child*

Between Father

HOW TO BECOME

and Child

THE KIND OF FATHER
YOU WANT TO BE

Dr. Ronald Levant and
John Kelly

Viking

VIKING
Published by the Penguin Group
Viking Penguin, a division of Penguin Books USA Inc., 40 West 23rd Street,
New York, New York 10010, U.S.A.
Penguin Books Ltd, 27 Wrights Lane,
London W8 5TZ, England
Penguin Books Australia Ltd, Ringwood,
Victoria, Australia
Penguin Books Canada Ltd, 2801 John Street,
Markham, Ontario, Canada L3R 1B4
Penguin Books (N.Z.) Ltd, 182–190 Wairau Road,
Auckland 10, New Zealand

Penguin Books Ltd, Registered Offices:
Harmondsworth, Middlesex, England

First published in 1989 by Viking Penguin, a division of
Penguin Books USA Inc.
Published simultaneously in Canada

10 9 8 7 6 5 4 3 2 1

Copyright © Ronald Levant and John Kelly, 1989
All rights reserved

LIBRARY OF CONGRESS CATALOGING IN PUBLICATION DATA
Levant, Ronald F.
  Between father and child.
  Bibliography: p.
  1. Fathers.   2. Parenting.   I. Kelly, John, 1945–
II. Title.
HQ756.L46   1989   649'.1   88-40414
ISBN 0-670-82805-X

Printed in the United States of America
Set in Garamond No. 3
Designed by Beth Tondreau Design

To our families

Authors' Note

The men you will meet in this book are composite portraits. Their experiences have been drawn from the experiences of many men who have attended the Fatherhood Project in the last ten years.

The names, backgrounds, and physical descriptions of the composites have all been changed to protect the privacy of the men whose stories provide the basis for these composites.

Acknowledgments

The Fatherhood Project, upon which this book is based, grew out of an applied research program directed by Dr. Levant at Boston University from 1975 to 1988. The program was concerned with strengthening the family, and produced psycho-educational preventive programs for foster parents, working parents, single parents, stepparents, in addition to the program for fathers. The research program was inspired by the theories of Carl R. Rogers. In addition, the work of people such as Thomas Gordon, Robert Carkhuff, Bernard and Louise Guerney, Allen Ivey, and Norman Kagan was influential in conceptualizing various aspects of the program.

It is also important to acknowledge the scores of students who helped develop the program over the thirteen-year period of its existence. Many students participated in the program, but those who did doctoral dissertation research deserve mention: Paul Slobodian, Susan Slattery, Milton Jay, Mark Geer, Nancy Haffey, Joel Kanigsberg, Wendy Nelson, and Elizabeth Tarshis. We particularly want to acknowledge the contributions of Greg Doyle, whose dissertation laid the foundation for the Fatherhood Project.

Next, we would like to acknowledge the contributions of Joseph Pleck, who provided a home for the germination of the Fatherhood Project at the Wellesley College Center for Research on Women in 1980, and who provided continuous assistance along the way.

We also want to acknowledge the support and encouragement of faculty colleagues at Boston University, including Eileen Nickerson, Ralph Mosher, Gene Bocknek, Oliva Espin, Joe Reimer, Kathy Vaughan, Jerry Fain, and Don Davies.

Finally, we would like to express our deep gratitude to the fathers who participated in our workshops. Through participating in a limited way in their struggles to learn new roles and create new family lives, we learned an incalculable amount about fathering, parenting, men, and families.

Contents

Between Father and Child

Introduction:
The New Father's Complaint

At 4:00 p.m. on this warm Monday in early September, the printout sheet I've been waiting for all day arrives from the university's computer center. It contains a list of the six men who will be in my section of the Fatherhood Project's Autumn Skills Training Program at Boston University. Over the past three weeks, each of the men on the list has been in my office for an hour-long interview, and from what I remember about each, aside from their membership in my new section, they have little in common. There's a bus driver and an advertising executive on the list, a computer salesman and a marketing manager, a baseball fan and a New Age music enthusiast, a divorced man and several who are happily married, a few men who are in their very early thirties and others who are in their mid-forties.

In a way, though, the diversity of the list tells its own story and it's an important, inspiring, even historic one. It's the story of the New Father and how deeply he and everything he represents have touched American men of all ages, occupations, and backgrounds. On any other subject American men speak in a hundred million different, often querulous voices, but for the past ten years on the subject of parenting, like the men on my list, they've spoken in a single loud and clear voice, and what it's been saying is "I want to change the terms of the father-child relationship from distant, wary, and respectful to warm, open, intimate, and tender." If you've been listening carefully to this voice, however (which is to say, if you've been listening carefully to yourself and your friends), you also know that, of late, a new note of hesitancy and self-doubt has crept into it.

It isn't that men are beginning to question their commitment to the New Father ideal or their dream of recasting the father-child relationship into a more intimate mold, but that today more and more men are questioning their ability to translate these goals into reality. "I'm finding I don't know how to be the kind of father I want to be" is a complaint heard with increasing frequency these days in offices, union halls, locker rooms—wherever men meet to talk.

The source of this complaint is easy enough to identify. While you and men like you want to create a new kind of father—one who is more representative of who you are and the times you live in—nothing in the male experience, upbringing, or parenting tradition has prepared you to be this sensitive, nurturing, responsive, tender, funny, warm figure. So when you try to be him, you end up, like the six men on my list, a little frustrated, a little doubtful, and very puzzled by your inability to be the father you want to be.

This book will give you the skills you need to be that dad. They were developed by my colleagues and myself at the Fatherhood Project of Boston University, and while they are designed to fit the masculine sensibility and parenting style, they are not specifically paternal skills. The kind of thoughtful, sensitive parenting they were created to promote is essential to *all* happy, loving, intimate parent-child relationships. So, in a sense, the techniques you'll find in the pages that follow are as relevant—and as potentially beneficial—to mothers as to fathers.

What makes them more pertinent to men is that men's upbringing—unlike women's—doesn't promote the kinds of communication qualities that make a child think, "Boy, Dad's someone I can really talk to." So no matter how hard they try, when they sit down to talk to their kids, most men unwittingly make the kinds of communication missteps that leave a child thinking, "I should have talked to Mom instead."

Exhibit A of the paternal misstep phenomenon is the inappropriate praise syndrome. The child says, "Dad, I hate my hair," and the father, being unfamiliar with the ways children communicate, misinterprets this remark as a request for praise, and so ends up giving the child what she doesn't want (a praising statement like "Well, I think your hair looks terrific"), instead of what she does want. (For the correct answer, see Chapter 1.)

Exhibit B of the misstep phenomenon is the "Yes, you will, mister" syndrome. The child says, "No, I won't," to a paternal request, and again, being unfamiliar with the ways a child communicates, Dad misinterprets this remark as an act of angry defiance, and so ends up getting into a fight that could have been avoided if he'd known how to read his child's "no" correctly. (See Chapter 5 for help.)

Exhibit C of the misstep phenomenon is the interjection syndrome. The child raises a concern in a statement like "Dad, I'm worried about my new science teacher." And instead of addressing the concern, Dad interjects his own concern by saying, "Well, you'd be less worried if you studied a little harder." (For a remedy, see Chapter 3.)

By the time you finish this book, you'll know how to avoid these missteps and you'll also know:

- How to read your child's hidden thoughts and feelings.
- How to avoid common father-child communications problems like the Tin Man, Rubber Band, and Mixed Messenger Syndromes, and the Yes-Dad-I-Do-No-Dad-I-Don't-Want-to-Talk trap.
- How to say no softly but effectively.
- How to talk to your child about important subjects like sex and drugs.
- How to resolve father-child conflicts in a way that strengthens rather than undermines the father-child relationship.
- How to use conversations to prevent common forms of childhood acting out like impulsivity, aggressiveness, and overeating.
- How to be a sympathetic listener.

By the time you finish the book, you'll also know how to do something else even more important: you'll know how to say, in deed as well as in voice, the three words that lie at the heart of every happy parent-child relationship: "I understand you." Traditionally, fathers—even New Fathers—have associated these words with a knowledge of a son's or daughter's interests and inclinations—knowing, for example, that Billy likes baseball, or Melissa is interested in computer science—and that kind of knowledge does represent a form of paternal understanding, but the kind of understanding that keeps a child returning to Dad and keeps him talking to Dad, long after he's run out of things to say about his special interest, involves another, deeper quality: the ability to make a youngster feel that when he says, "Dad, I'm mad (or sad or glad)," Dad knows exactly how those emotions feel to him; and that when he says, "Dad, I have a problem with Friend A (or Teacher B)," Dad knows just how he sees his problem with Friend A or Teacher B.

In other words, it involves the ability to make the child feel Dad understands him so well that Dad can step inside his mind and see his problems or emotions the way he sees them. This is the deepest and truest form of understanding one human being can extend to another, and it has a magical effect on the parent-child relationship for pretty much the same reason it has a magical effect on any other kind of relationship. Dad's understanding validates the child because it shows that Dad takes him and his opinions and concerns seriously enough to try to see them from his perspective. And even more important, Dad's understanding creates a special kind of connection, one that fosters such a sense of attunement that the child always feels himself inside the charmed circle of father-child understanding.

At the Fatherhood Project, we call this kind of understanding *perspective-taking,* and in one way or another, the skills we've developed for our program fathers are designed to foster it. The first set is known as *Other-Directed* skills, and as its strategies, *Listening to Content* and *Understanding Hidden Messages,* are mastered, a father discovers he's able to identify what's on his child's mind even when the child doesn't tell him what he's thinking or feeling.

The second set of skills is known as *Self-directed,* and as this set's components, *Self-awareness* and *Self-expression,* are mastered, a father also finds he is able to do something he couldn't do before: set aside his own preconceptions and look at his child's thoughts and feelings from the child's perspective. *Resolution Negotiation,* the program's fifth skill, also fosters an ability rare among men today: the capacity to *fairly* balance paternal concerns against the child's.

In their turn, these perceptions lead to several other important discoveries. Suddenly the father finds himself addressed in full paragraphs instead of monosyllables, and he finds that now, when he says, "How about a ball game tonight?" or "Do you want to go to McDonald's for dinner?," more often than not, the answer is "Yes, I'd love to, Dad." And what pleases him just as much, he finds that now, when he says, "Please lower the stereo" or "Please pick up your stuff," he only has to ask once. And what usually pleases him most of all, he discovers that now, when he raises important subjects like sex and drug use, instead of trying to duck, his child says, "Fine, Dad, let's talk."

These are the kinds of discoveries every New Father wants to make today, and as you master the skills in the pages that follow, you'll find yourself making them as readily as the six men on my list.

Part I
The Skills

A: Other-Directed Skills

The skills in group one are designed to help you identify your child's thoughts and feelings. The two skills in this category are:

1. Listening to Content
2. Understanding Hidden Messages

1
How to Talk to a Child

Keri Pullio is fifteen years old, a sophomore at Somerville High School, and she likes: Vinnie Orsini, Somerville's starting quarterback; stone-washed jeans; spiked hair; her best friend, Gina Plassio (sometimes); and her father, Dave (also sometimes).

Dave Pullio is forty-three years old, a bus driver for the MBTA, and he likes the Knights of Columbus, the Boston Red Sox, Vinnie Orsini (sometimes), and Gina Plassio (also sometimes).

About Keri herself, Dave's feelings are more complex. He loves her, of course, and despite the way she behaves sometimes, he knows she loves him. But Dave does wonder why Keri, who can spend hours on the phone discussing Vinnie's latest haircut with Gina, or hours in the kitchen discussing eye shadow with her mother, can't sit and talk to him anywhere about anything for more than three minutes at a time without becoming antsy, exasperated, or angry or—usually—all three at once.

Sometimes Dave thinks he's the problem: "Everyone

knows that girls find it easier to talk to their mothers," he'll tell himself. Other times, he thinks Keri's the problem. "No one's ever actually talked to a teenage girl," he'll say. But mostly what Dave thinks is that, for some unaccountable reason, his orderly little universe of Red Sox games and Knights of Columbus outings has been invaded by a creature as irresistible as a smile and incomprehensible as a Black Hole. And one Tuesday evening, early last September, Dave described the hazards of living with this creature to the five other men who had joined him in Room 310 at Boston University for the first meeting of Section C of the Fatherhood Project's fall group.

One of the little rituals of these first meetings is an introduction. I ask each man to tell us his name, the names and ages of his children, and to explain briefly to the rest of the group why he's joined the project. Dave, who was the first father I called on this evening, began as requested. He squirmed out of his chair, stated his name, and said that he had two children, a seventeen-year-old named Dominick and a fifteen-year-old named Keri.

He also said he was upset. And when I asked him why, he replied by giving the group a classic example of a problem nearly every father has encountered at one time or another: The Yes-Dad-I-Do-No-Dad-I-Don't-Want-to-Talk Syndrome. After giving every indication that he's bursting to tell you something, and, often, after actually beginning to tell you what it is, the child inexplicably lapses into silence and withdraws.

Sometimes the withdrawal is relatively quiet and discreet—you and the conversation suddenly just seem boring; other times it is dramatic and violent, accompanied by flashing lights and heavy piano music. But whatever form it takes, the withdrawal almost always leaves its paternal victims wondering, "Why do kids behave the way they do?"

In Dave's case, the events which led him to ask this question of himself had occurred the previous Saturday night when a tearful Keri had plopped down beside him on the couch, and after weeks of yeses, nos and uh-huhs, suddenly began telling him about a dance she and Gina and Vinnie had been to earlier that evening. The gist of her tale was that Vinnie had hardly spoken to her all night, but danced with Gina three times. And from the unguarded way Keri talked about her pain and anger at being shut out, it was clear to Dave that this time she had decided to confide in him, which both touched and pleased him.

"I thought finally, after all this time, Keri was turning to her old dad for a little help," he said. "But when I told her, 'Look, Pumpkin, I know you feel terrible, but this isn't the end of the world,' Keri looked at me funny. And when I said, 'Besides, I think you're a hundred times prettier than Gina,' she actually seemed mad. And when I said, 'Lots of boys would be proud to have you as a girlfriend,' Keri got so upset she threw herself on the couch and began yelling, 'Go away, Dad, just go away. I don't want to talk anymore.' I felt like I'd been hit by a truck."

Paul Cronin, the next member of the group to introduce himself, also had some experience with the Yes-Dad-I-Do-No-Dad-I-Don't-Want-to-Talk Syndrome. But in his family, its chief perpetrator wasn't his teenage daughter, a seventeen-year-old named Colleen, but his fourteen-year-old son, Tim.

"I feel about Tim the way Dave feels about Keri," Paul said. "He operates on a different wavelength than the rest of us. The other morning's a good example. At breakfast Tim said he was worried about a gymnastics meet he had that afternoon because he hadn't practiced his back flips. This, I should point out, is not unprecedented behavior for Timothy. But I know how kids can tie themselves up in knots over things like gymnastics meets and I didn't want Tim upsetting himself. So I said, 'Tim, don't worry, you're going to be the star of the show.'

"Well, from the way he jumped, you'd think I'd just leaned across the table and hit him over the head with a hammer. Tim got very huffy, snapped, 'I'm not the star of the show, Dad. I'm just a regular kid who's in it.' Then he grabbed his books and marched off without even saying goodbye."

The reason the Yes-Dad-I-Do-No-Dad-I-Don't-Want-to-Talk Syndrome seems so puzzling—and painful—to men like Paul and Dave is that the child's behavior appears totally gratuitous. Dad extends himself by offering some kind, comforting words, and instead of thanking him, the youngster abruptly shuts the door in his face. However, reactions like Keri's and Tim's aren't as mysterious or incomprehensible as they look. Most of the sudden squalls of anger that can make a boy or girl seem as irrational as a force of nature really are just a child's way of saying, "I don't feel understood." And the reasons dads—even dads like Paul and Dave, who are trying very hard to be reassuring and comforting—often find themselves caught up in these squalls is that most men don't know how to talk to a child in a way that makes him or her feel understood.

The goal of this book and the program it's based on is to show you how to do that. And as we move from chapter to chapter, you'll learn how to do it in increasingly complex and difficult situations. So that by the end of the book you'll know how to tell your child, "I understand you," even when he doesn't understand himself, or when you disagree with him, or when the two of you find your-selves in outright conflict. But in this chapter we're going to begin with a very basic form of paternal understand-ing, though also a very important one, because it is linked to the Yes-Dad-I-Do-No-Dad-I-Don't-Want-to-Talk Syn-drome. It's how to tell a youngster, "I'm ready to listen," when he says, "Dad, I have a problem."

In terms of feeling understood, Dad's reassurance that he'll listen carefully represents the child's emotional bot-tom line. Even a boy or girl who's bursting to tell you about Vinnie or Gina or about the gymnastics meet won't, or will suddenly change his mind, if he feels you don't understand him. And there are three reasons why dads have trouble providing such understanding: Either they listen to themselves instead of to the child; they respond inaccurately to the concerns they hear voiced; or they ig-nore the reactions their responses produce.

Accordingly, *Listening to Content,* the project's first skill, is designed to show you how to avoid these missteps by helping you to:

- correctly identify the issue or problem your young-ster is raising;
- respond in a way that lets the youngster know Dad understands why he or she is feeling upset or worried;
- check out the accuracy of your replies.

Identification, the first step, is important for the simple reason that a child who comes to you with a worry or problem won't talk about it until he feels you've accurately understood that problem or concern. And while pinpoint-ing it may sound simple, especially when a youngster states it as directly and clearly as Tim Cronin and Keri Pullio did, there are two ways a man's own preconceptions can make a child feel Dad's misidentified him.

One is when Dad surrenders to the siren call of his paternal guardian angel, Perfect Dad. Perfect Dad is an amalgam of every parenting rule a man has ever heard, and because all those rules say the best way to deal with an upset or troubled child is to offer immediate praise and reassurance, that's what most men do. When they hear a problem or concern voiced, they'll say, "Don't worry" or "You'll feel better" or "Well, I like your hair."

These sentiments are always heartfelt. But since to a child who's just raised a very specific problem they usually sound like non sequiturs, they're also a leading cause of the Yes-Dad-I-Do-No-Dad-I-Don't-Want-to-Talk Syndrome. Dave Pullio's and Paul Cronin's responses are cases in point. Dave's "I think you're a hundred times prettier than Gina" and Paul's "You're going to be the star of the show" are both *perfect* Perfect Dad remarks. Each is well meant and seemingly soothing. But neither gave Keri and Tim what they wanted. Keri said she wanted to talk about her problem with her friend. Tim indicated that he wanted to discuss his worries about the gymnastics show. And when they both got unasked-for praise, instead, they both concluded what kids usually do in their situation: "Dad doesn't know what I'm saying. I guess there's no point talking to him."

Prejudgment is the other form of paternal preconception that can lead a child to this conclusion. In this case, though, the culprit isn't Perfect Dad but the man's own suspicions. Over time, he comes to think everything his youngster says is a veiled request for money, clothes, or another ride to the mall, and so he begins interpreting everything he hears on the basis of this wariness and not on what's actually said to him.

A story Sam Aberjanassi, another member of the new fall group, told is a case in point. After introducing himself, Sam said that the night's discussion had made him wonder about a conversation he'd had with his six-year-old, Ricky, after Tommy Logan, Ricky's best friend, got a new two-wheeler with training wheels. "Ricky still has a tricycle," Sam said, "and when he told me, 'Dad, I'm worried. I think Tommy's going to learn to ride his new two-wheeler before me,' I thought, 'Uh-oh, Ricky's going to ask me for a new two-wheeler!' "

"Did he?" I asked.

"No, but our conversation didn't last that long, Ron. After I reminded Rick that I'd just spent a hundred dollars on a new Nintendo set, he said, 'Okay, Dad,' and walked away. I've been congratulating myself ever since for my preemptive strike. But now I'm puzzled. Do you think I misjudged? Did Ricky really just want to talk to me about Tommy?"

I told Sam that was a distinct possibility. And I also told him it's just as likely that when Ricky heard his intention misidentified, he concluded what Tim and Keri concluded: "Dad's listening to himself, not me," and so he did what they did: withdrew.

The best way to avoid missteps like Sam's—and Dave's and Paul's—is to state the child's problem back to him or her. This technique, which we call *paraphrasing,* is the second step in Listening to Content, and what makes it an effective antidote to the Yes-Dad-I-Do-No-Dad-I-Don't-Want-to-Talk Syndrome is that it tells the youngster very clearly and directly that you've identified his problem correctly and are ready to listen. In Ricky Aberjanassi's case, an example of a paraphrase that would have gotten this important message across is "Ricky, you're worried that Tommy's going to learn to ride a two-wheeler before you."

In Keri Pullio's case, such an example would be "Pumpkin, you're really upset that Vinnie and Gina paid so much attention to each other tonight, aren't you?" And in Tim Cronin's, "Tim, you're worried about what you're going to do this afternoon because you didn't practice for the show."

Adults don't normally talk this way, so I suspect paraphrasing will sound strange to many readers. But to a child, restating a concern is the emotional equivalent of flashing a green light. It reassures her that you've identified what she's said and, even more important, it tells her you aren't going to interrupt, interrogate, or interpret her, but are going to sit back and let her tell you about her problem or worry the way she sees it. And when a child knows that Dad's trying to look at her problem from her perspective, she'll take down the bar, unlock the door, and put the light on for Dad.

Occasionally, a father will object that the technique sounds too direct, too blunt—too unkind, really. But that's only because Perfect Dad's accustomed men to associate paternal comforting and soothing with bland, no-fault phrases like "Don't worry." To a child, paraphrasing sounds very kind because, along with acknowledging her perspective, it also provides her with a form of paternal validation. It tells her Dad respects her right to feel the way she does about, say, Vinnie and Gina.

Offering immediate praise and reassurance may make Dad feel better, but telling a youngster "You'll feel better tomorrow" or "I really like your hair" has the additional disadvantage of making him feel that Dad's trying to talk him out of his feelings instead of trying to accept and understand them.

John Uterhof, the next member of the group to introduce himself, raised an important point about paraphrasing: sometimes a child will pile three or four different concerns into a single statement. "My nine-year-old, Eric, does this quite a bit," John said, "and my sixteen-year-old, Margery, even more. The other day, for example, she said to me, 'Dad, I hate my hair. All the kids will think I look like a dip.' Which of these two different concerns should I have replied to?"

In one form or another, John's question frequently comes up in discussions of paraphrasing, because children do tend to lump different issues together—especially when they're confused about what's really bothering them. And since singling out one or another of their concerns for a reply often only deepens their confusion, the best policy to follow in such cases is to restate the child's *entire message*. In the case of the teenager who says, "Dad, I don't like my boss. I'm thinking about getting a new job," for example, an appropriate response would be "You'd like to get another job. You find your boss hard to get along with."

In the case of Margery Uterhof's complaint, an appropriate restatement would be a phrase like "You sound worried. You don't think your hair will be a hit with your friends?"

This remark includes both concerns, so it opens the door to the kind of discussion that will allow Margery to decide which of the two issues is bothering her more this morning, her hair or her friends.

One word of advice, though.

Often, before your child says a word, you'll know that

it's the kids or her boss who is bothering her, and what she should do about her problem. Keep this information to yourself.

The discoveries that mean the most to us—in other words, the discoveries we're most likely to learn from and act on—are the ones we make for ourselves. And one of the chief purposes of paraphrasing in particular, and Listening to Content in general, is to open the door to the kind of thoughtful, intimate discussion where such self-discoveries are made. As the child talks through her feelings, sooner or later she'll discover whether what's bothering her this morning is her friends or her boss—and what to do about it.

Your job in this process is to be a facilitator. You should offer clarifying comments or questions when needed and advice when asked for, but you should let your boy or girl be the discoverer.

Let's see how well you understand the principles of paraphrasing now. Imagine that your daughter's just said, "Dad, I can't stand Lisa anymore. She complains all the time. It's driving me crazy." Which of the following four statements most accurately restates her concern:

1. Lisa's a nice girl; you shouldn't talk that way about her.
2. Honey, I've always believed if you can't say something nice about a person you shouldn't say anything at all.
3. If you start ignoring Lisa, she's going to feel hurt.
4. You don't like Lisa anymore; you think she complains too much.

Perfect Dad will tell you to pick 1 and 3 because they sound pleasant and inoffensive. But they also share one problem: neither addresses the real issues.

Your daughter wouldn't bring up Lisa's complaining if it didn't bother her. And while it may turn out that it bothers her for a trivial reason, it may also turn out that it bothers her for an important one. Lisa may even be complaining about her. In either case, your daughter won't tell you until you first tell her you understand that what she wants to talk about is Lisa's behavior toward her and not her behavior toward Lisa. And the only reply that does that is the last—and also most direct—one: "You don't like Lisa any more; you think she complains too much."

After learning why Lisa's complaining is so irritating, some paternal advice very likely will be in order. But here as well avoid exhortations and admonitions. Aside from sounding unhelpful, statements like "Why don't you give Lisa another chance?" or "No one's perfect" in effect say, "I don't accept your right to be annoyed at Lisa"; and that, in effect, tells a child, "I don't accept your right to have feelings of your own." A well-placed suggestion like "Why don't you take Lisa aside and talk to her?" will allow you to avoid this hazard and at the same time give your youngster some advice she can use.

Let's look at another example now. This time, imagine that your son's just said, "Dad, I feel bad; I studied hard and I only got a B on my math test." Which of the following four statements would best restate his message:

1. If you wanted a better grade, you should have studied harder.
2. B is a perfectly respectable grade. I wouldn't feel upset if I were you.

3. Cheer up; this weekend we're going camping.
4. You feel bad because you didn't do as well as you wanted to.

Perfect Dad's introduced a new tactic in this list of choices. Replies 1 and 2 embody his belief that, in every instance, a father should be praising and reassuring. But he knows that sometimes such "bucking up" not only can sound beside the point to an upset child; it can annoy him. So in response 3, Perfect Dad's presented a new ploy: get the disappointed youngster's mind off his disappointment by reminding him of something pleasant—an upcoming camping trip.

We call this tactic *diversion,* and it has the same two drawbacks as unasked-for praise. It creates an atmosphere of misunderstanding and rejection. You leave the child thinking, "Dad doesn't know or want to find out what I'm feeling." And, equally important, it doesn't work. Children are very single-minded about their problems, and when they are burning up with disappointment about a performance on a math test, the only response that will satisfy them is one that directly addresses that disappointment. And in this case that's reply 4: "You feel bad because you didn't do as well as you wanted to."

Checking, the third step in Listening to Content, is designed to help you deal with a problem that occasionally confronts even masters of this skill. Despite your best effort to sound understanding, the child still begins slipping over into the No-Dad-I-Don't-Want-to-Talk part of the syndrome. Usually a youngster who's heading in this direction will signal his intention through facial expressions and body language. A change from an intent expression to one that is bored, uninterested, or guarded is one such signal. Another is a sudden, severe case of the antsys. The child who starts shifting from right to left in his chair, then from left to right, or who keeps crossing and uncrossing his legs or folding and unfolding his arms, or who doesn't know what to do with his hands usually is a child who is thinking, "Dad hasn't heard what I said. I think it's time for me to leave."

Inaccurate and inappropriate paternal paraphrases are a leading reason for such sudden changes of heart. On occasion a boy or girl will even come out and tell you directly, "Dad, you've misunderstood me." And if you listen carefully to the way you're corrected, often you can tell how great your misunderstanding is. Usually, if your restatement is close to the mark, the child will say, "Yes, but . . ." or "It's almost that" or "It's a lot like you say, except . . ." If you're considerably off, she'll respond with a vague generality like "It's sort of like that" or "It's kinda the way you say, Dad," and if you're way off, she'll either say flatly, "No, you have it wrong," or, more typically, she'll lapse into silence.

A statement like "It sounds as if I've misunderstood you; why don't you explain it to me one more time?" will let the boy or girl know that you've made an error and want to correct it. And having been given that reassurance, she'll sit back, relax, and let you try a second time.

Another leading cause of such sudden changes of heart is *paternal body language*. The way a man sits, looks, crosses or uncrosses his legs often tells a boy or girl as much about Dad's readiness to listen as his words do. And because a man's upbringing doesn't teach him to pay much attention to this aspect of communication, often when he sits down to talk to his child he ignores the four forms of body language that say, "I'm ready to listen."

The first, *getting on your child's level,* involves sitting down directly in front of the child. You know you're doing it correctly when your eyes and shoulders are more or less level with your son's or daughter's. This says, "Dad's in," as clearly and firmly as breaking eye contact, intense staring, and a shifty gaze say, "Dad's out." The *tilt of your body* also makes an important statement. Leaning forward slightly says, "I'm interested," and leaning forward markedly says, "I'm very interested," while leaning back says, "I'm bored." *Body posture* in the form of a relaxed stance and uncrossed arms and legs will also convey a willingness to listen. And shutting off the TV and radio, and eliminating all other distractions underline that willingness.

Simple as checking and the other steps in Listening to Content may be, welding them together into an effective communications tool takes experience and practice; one of the ways we provide project dads with both is through a technique we call role playing. It involves having two group members—one playing a father, the other a child—use the skill we've talked about in session to solve a real-life problem. And what makes the technique such a valuable teaching method is that it dramatizes a skill's uses in a way that words alone cannot. A case in point is the role play that ended the fall group's first session.

Its subject was the story that had opened the session, the Keri Pullio–Vinnie Orsini–Gina Plassio triangle, and its two participants were Dave Pullio and George Phelan. Dave agreed to play himself, and I selected George, who had introduced himself a few minutes earlier, to play Keri because in describing his two youngsters, Megan, eight, and Billy, thirteen, he'd revealed a flair for the dramatic.

"Dave," I said, "imagine that Keri has just told you, 'Dad, I feel terrible. Vinnie danced with Gina three times tonight.' How would you use Listening to Content to draw her out and help her talk through her upset?"

Father: Gina and Vinnie made you feel bad tonight, didn't they, Pumpkin?

Child: Yes, they did, Dad. They're both rats. Vinnie hardly said anything to me all night and that dip Gina was like a rug over him. Why would she do that, Dad? She knows how much I like Vinnie.

Father: It sounds like Gina's the one you're really mad at, Pumpkin.

Child: I am, Dad. Vinnie's a little dumb but he's cute. But that Gina! What a tramp. You should have seen her tonight, Dad. She was practically exploding out of her dress. I don't know how she got into it. Yes, I do: she wears a girdle. Imagine that she's not even sixteen yet and she wears a girdle. She's going to be an even bigger tub than her mother.

Father: What do you think you ought to do about Gina, Keri?

Child: I don't know, Dad. She's supposed to be my best friend. She can't pull this stuff on me. You know what I'm going to do? I'm going to talk to her tomorrow at school.

Father: Good idea, Pumpkin.

Dave's and George's role play is a good example not only of Listening to Content's strengths but also of its limitations. You can only use it in instances where the child's openness and directness about a concern give you something to paraphrase. Keri did this when she said,

"Dad, I feel terrible. Vinnie danced with Gina three times tonight." And so did Tim Cronin when he said, "Dad, I'm worried about the gymnastics show."

Their remarks are examples of what we call straight-forward statements, and whenever they are used, Listening to Content is the appropriate skill to employ. But as Roger Levine, the last member of the group to introduce himself, noted, often a youngster won't tell you directly what's bothering him. "My eight-year-old, Max, is an example," Roger said. "I'll know from his mopiness that he's upset, but when I ask him what's wrong, he'll shake his head and say, 'Nothing, Dad.' "

I told Roger that Max's behavior is typical of a child with a hidden message. Hidden messages involve issues the youngster isn't able to articulate clearly to himself or to anyone else. In the next chapter, we'll look at how to deal with them.

2

How to Talk to a Child When He Doesn't Know What He Wants to Say

I used to think that those angry black storm clouds you see hovering over fathers in cartoon strips were an expression of artistic imagination until I walked into the coatroom a few minutes before the second session and saw one hovering half a foot over George Phelan's spiked hair. George's cloud was every bit as dark and menacing as the ones I'd seen in the strips, but so big it nearly knocked over Dave Pullio, who'd walked in right behind me.

"Uh-oh, look at George here," Dave said as he pressed against the coatroom wall to give George and his cloud room to pass. "What has you so upset tonight, guy?"

George frowned and flung a single furious epithet across the coatroom. "Billy!"

Dave suddenly looked concerned. "George, your boy. Is he sick?"

"No, Dave, he's not sick; he's got me sick. Sunday night he made a first-class fool of me and he considerately did it in front of one of his friends. A boy named Seth."

George stopped, sighed, then explained what had happened. "At dinner, Seth and Billy were talking about U2. You know them, don't you? They're one of the new rock groups. Anyway, I thought why don't I let these kids listen to some real music. I'll play them one of my George Winston tapes. He's a big name in harmonics—it's a kind of New Age music.

"Well, Seth seemed to enjoy the music. But Billy practically fell over himself smirking and putting me down. First, he said New Age music was stupid; then he said people who eat Product 19 are stupid, and then he said that since I like New Age music and I eat Product 19, I must be the stupidest thing going."

I noticed George's storm cloud had begun shaking violently, so violently, in fact, that a moment later it burst with a tremendous thunderclap.

"Dammit, Ron, where does Billy get off treating me like the Thousand-Year-Old Man? Besides, even if I was Father Time, I'm still Billy's dad and you don't humiliate your dad, and you especially don't humiliate him in front of other people. What got into him the other night, Ron? He's never behaved like that before."

"If this is a first, George, the answer to your question probably lies with Seth, not Billy," I said. "What kind of boy is Seth?"

"Bow your head when you mention his name, Ron. Billy's crew thinks Seth could raise himself from the dead if he wanted."

"And Billy's relationship with him?"

"Frankly?"

"Frankly."

"Seth considers Billy his Gunga Din."

"I think you've just answered your own question, George. Billy's belittling of you is a sign he has some anxieties about Seth. In a word, Seth intimidates him."

George shook his head.

"Why didn't Billy just tell me that?"

In one form or another, I've heard George's question a hundred different times. And in one way or another, the father who asks it is always saying the same thing: "Help, I've just been blindsided by the *Hidden Message Phenomenon*." This is the second type of communication children use, and what makes it such a common source of paternal whiplash as well as perplexity is that it is also behind many of the behaviors fathers find upsetting and hurtful.

What distinguishes the phenomenon from the straightforward statements we looked at in the last chapter—and also what makes it so puzzling—is that unlike Keri Pullio and Tim Cronin, who said what they meant, children with a hidden message don't, and most often they don't because they can't. Their hidden message touches on the kinds of complex concerns their five-, ten-, or fifteen-year-old selves still lack the awareness and knowledge to clearly identify and articulate.

Typically, these complex concerns also touch threatening or ego-deflating issues like intimidating peers and problematic boyfriends and girlfriends. So, in many cases, hidden messages remain hidden, too, because the child would just as soon leave the issues in them unexamined.

What makes the phenomenon a major source of behavioral as well as communicative problems is that big issues like intimidating peers and problematic boyfriends produce big emotions like fear and anxiety. And while talking the issue through will usually assuage the feelings it's producing, hidden issues can't be talked about. So the emotions they produce tend to sit there and grow until finally they get so big they begin spilling over into the child's behavior.

Technically, this spillover effect is known as acting out. One example of how hidden messages generate this effect is the teenager who is angry at her boyfriend for breaking a Christmas Day date but doesn't know that. This happened to a daughter of one of our program dads, and because the youngster couldn't explain why she was angry to herself or to anyone else, her anger grew and grew, until finally it spilled over onto her father, who on Christmas morning was furiously denounced as a rat for not having spent enough on her Christmas present.

Billy Phelan's put-down is another example of the spillover effect. Billy's hidden message the night of Seth's visit was "My friend intimidates me." But since Billy didn't know that and, hence, couldn't talk about it, his anxieties about Seth grew until they required an outlet, which Billy provided by putting down his father.

Reactions like Billy's and that angry teenager's are why an important part of this chapter's skill, *Understanding Hidden Messages,* involves learning how to tell what a youngster means when he can't—or won't—tell you what he means. Imagine how good Billy Phelan would have felt if his dad could have put his finger on Billy's worries about Seth, gently lifted them up into the light, and assuaged them. The dad who can do this is telling his boy or girl in a very special way, "I understand you," and, just as important, he's helping that boy or girl—and himself—avoid the kind of acting out that victimized George Phelan.

Such hidden-message-related acting out is so common that it featured prominently in two other stories I heard during the second meeting. The first was told by a very upset-looking Sam Aberjanassi, who wondered whether his son Ricky's recent hit-and-run attack on his friend Tommy Logan was inspired by a hidden message.

The attack had occurred a few days earlier. Ricky had suddenly shot out of the Aberjanassi driveway on his tricycle while Tommy was riding by on his two-wheeler, and had knocked Tommy off his bike. What made Sam think a hidden message might be involved is that a week before the incident, Ricky had said to him, "Dad, Tommy's learned to ride his two-wheeler without training wheels"; then added, for no apparent reason, "You know what? I hate my bike." "Do you think there was a hidden message in his remark?" Sam asked.

I told him yes. "Like Billy Phelan, it sounds as if Ricky had a big unidentified issue—'I'm jealous of Tommy Logan because he can ride a two-wheeler and I can't'—he couldn't talk about. So his jealousy of Tommy turned to anger and the angrier he got, the bigger the bull's-eye on Tommy's forehead grew, until finally Ricky exploded and did what angry males—and in particular half-socialized six- and seven-year-old angry males—do; he acted out his anger in violence."

The second story was told by John Uterhof, who said he also thought his daughter, Margery, was suffering from a case of hidden-message-related acting out. But his tale illustrates another aspect of this phenomenon. Sometimes unidentified issues produce an inner form of acting out. Instead of finding a Tommy Logan to lash out at, the child aims the upset produced by the hidden message at herself. And this is what John thought Margery was doing with her suddenly developed habit of binge eating.

"The eating began after the breakup with her boyfriend, Timmy," John explained, "and it's very out of character for Margery. She's a pretty weight-conscious young lady. My wife, Joan, and I think she's punishing herself. She was pretty tough on Tim at the end, and we suspect she's beating herself up for that now by doing something she knows she'll hate herself for, getting fat."

Since out-of-character behaviors like Margery Uterhof's are one of the ways hidden messages announce themselves, John's story serves as a good introduction to *Identification,* the first step in the program's second skill. Before you can deal with a hidden message, you have to know how to identify one, and, normally, such messages announce themselves in one of five ways—all of which, to varying degrees, are forms of acting out. The emotion generated by the hidden message has now grown to the point where it's begun spilling over into the child's attitude, concerns, or actions. And one of the most common of these spillover effects is the appearance of a new and usually very troubling *out-of-character* behavior, like Margery's binge eating.

Most often, these behaviors appear suddenly; the child's acting normally and in character one day, and the next day, abnormally and out of character. But sometimes out-of-character behaviors can also take the harder-to-detect, gradual-onset form. Stevie Stein, the son of a former program dad, is a case in point. Stevie's behavior didn't change dramatically from one day to the next or even from one month to the next. But over the course of a year, it altered in one significant and out-of-character way. Baseball-loving Stevie wasn't playing much ball anymore. His cutback was so gradual, though, it took a fortunate combination of circumstances, which included a banged fist and a phone call, for his dad, Robert, to spot it and the hidden messages behind it.

As a program father, Robert knew that *body language* is also a form of acting out that can signal a hidden message. So the night Stevie banged his fist on the table and said, "Dad, Rudy Micheau thinks I ought to play volleyball," Robert was pretty sure he was in the presence of a hidden message; and after he offered a few reflections, which is a technique we'll look at later in the chapter, Robert discovered he was right. Underneath the anger that had produced Stevie's banged fist was the message "Dad, Rudy told me to try volleyball because he thinks I'm a lousy first baseman." It wasn't until two weeks later, however, when he got a phone call from Rudy's apologetic father, that Robert realized how long his son had been harboring this particular hidden message.

"I haven't seen much of your boy at the ballpark over the past year," William Micheau said, "and I think my Rudy may be responsible. I don't know if Billy told you, but the two of them had a terrible argument last June that ended with Rudy's shouting, 'You're a lousy ballplayer, Stevie; you ought to try volleyball. It's a good game for girls.'"

One particularly noteworthy aspect of Stevie's story is the form of acting out he used. Normally, boys with hidden-message-related emotions express them by lashing out at other people the way Rick Aberjanassi lashed out at Tommy Logan. Stevie did what Margery Uterhof—and most girls—do; he internalized his anger. Instead of punishing Rudy, he punished himself by doing less and less of something he loved. And he probably would have continued on that course until finally he wasn't playing ball at all if Rudy hadn't kept on his case about the volleyball. But Rudy did, so, at a certain point, Stevie's acting out reverted to a more typically male form. His anger turned around and started heading outward, and if Robert hadn't caught the hidden message underneath it, it probably would have continued heading outward until Stevie's angry fist jumped from the table into Rudy Micheau's face.

Though a slammed fist is a pretty easy form of body language to read, hidden messages can also announce themselves more subtly. Gaze patterns are a case in point. You might think, for example, that the teenager whose eyes don't meet yours when she says, "Dad, I promise this is the last time you'll ever have to ask me to pick up my room," is simply bored by the subject of her room. But this kind of gaze aversion can also represent a subtle form of acting out. The teenager is unhappy with herself and, if you did what Robert Stein did and offered a few reflections, very likely underneath her unhappiness you'd find the hidden message, "Oh, God, am I ever going to learn to pick up my room without having to be asked four hundred times?"

Most dads probably would be content just to bring this thought up into the light. But—as we'll see a little later in the chapter—hidden messages often are interconnected in ways that can lead from an important message to a still more important one. So if you stopped at this initial message, you and the youngster wouldn't get to the even more important one under it, which very likely would be "Dad, the reason you have to keep asking me to pick up my room is that I don't think I'm grown-up enough to be a responsible person."

The fifteen-year-old whose eyes flit from you to her unmade bed to the empty container of Chinese takeout on the bureau when you ask her to pick up her room is using her eyes to act out a hidden message. But her shifty gaze is not saying, "Dad, I don't feel responsible"; it is saying, "Dad, some of your criticisms make me feel dumb," or to put it more directly, "Dad, some of your criticisms are humiliating."

The youngster who finds everything and everyone around him "dumb" or "stupid" or "creepy" or "dopey" also is acting out. But *repetition of certain key words in different contexts* represents a verbal form of the phenomenon, which signals the presence of hidden messages. The child's continual repetition of derogatory words or phrases expresses an inner dissatisfaction with himself, and if you lifted up that dissatisfaction and peeked underneath it, you'd almost always find a hidden message involving a recent defeat or failure.

Roger Levine's son, Max, is a case in point. When I mentioned repetition during the second session, Roger said that Max had gone through a repetitive period the previous summer when he didn't make his Little League team's final cut. "For two weeks after the cut, Max couldn't describe anything without attaching the adjective 'dumb' to it. I was dumb, Larry Bird was dumb, all his friends were dumb, even 'Alf,' his favorite TV show, was suddenly dumb."

Non sequiturs are the fourth form of acting out to signal a hidden message. The phrase means an "out-of-the-blue" remark, and while it may seem an odd term to apply to acting out, hidden messages frequently generate the kinds of feelings that lead to out-of-the-blue remarks. Ricky Aberjanassi's "Dad, I hate my bike" is an example. It was prompted not by a question from his dad but by Ricky's anger and jealousy of Tommy Logan's bike-riding skills.

Five-year-old Harry McCann offers another illustration. Twice in the course of a ten-minute soliloquy on Batman, Harry interrupted himself to ask his father, Ian,

"Dad, how far away is the movie you and Mom are going to tonight?" Harry's question didn't have much to do with Batman, but it had a great deal to do with his hidden message, which was "Dad, I'm anxious about the new baby-sitter who's coming tonight." And because Ian, who had been through the program, knew what non sequiturs like Harry's question signaled, he picked up on its hidden message the second time he was asked about the movie, and within a few minutes the two of them were talking not about Batman but about how worried Harry was by the prospect of having a new sitter.

The McCanns' story is also a good example of another form of acting out that can signal a hidden message, *emotional discrepancies*. When a child is burning up with a hidden-message-related emotion, often some of that emotion will slip into his words, creating a discrepancy between what's said and how it's said. Ian told me this was the other signal that alerted him to Harry's hidden message. "How far away is the movie you and Mom are going to see tonight?" is a pretty innocuous inquiry. But Harry's worries about his new sitter were so great that some of them slipped into his voice, turning his seemingly mundane question into a study in anxiety.

Once you know your child has a hidden message, the next step is to bring it up into the light where it can be identified and talked about. That's the goal of *Reflection,* the second step in Understanding Hidden Messages. It means reflecting back to him the *emotion* you see or hear in the child's body language, non sequiturs, out-of-character behaviors, dissonance, or repeated words. And to illustrate how the technique works, let's apply it to the remarks and behaviors Ricky Aberjanassi, Billy Phelan, and Max Levine used to signal their hidden messages.

Ricky's "Dad, I hate my bike" is a pretty angry statement, so the appropriate reflection for him would be "Rick, you sound mad this morning." Billy Phelan's out-of-character put-downs of his dad are a sign of anxiety, so the appropriate reflection for him would be one that referred to that anxiety, such as, "Gee, Billy, you sounded anxious last night" or, better still (we'll see why in a moment), "Gee, you didn't seem very relaxed at dinner the other night." For Max Levine, whose constant use of the word "dumb" signaled some self-esteem problems, the most appropriate reflection would be one that addressed those problems, like "Max, I hear a lot of dissatisfaction in your constant put-downs of everything as 'dumb.'"

Metaphorically speaking, a child's hidden messages are like a honeycomb of caves and such direct, straightforward paternal descriptions of mood and feeling facilitate his exploration of these caves in two important ways. One is by assuring him that wherever he goes, Dad will be right beside him.

Putting on a pith helmet and bush jacket and marching into the cave marked "Tommy" or "Seth" is a pretty intimidating prospect for a six- or sixteen-year-old—especially one who intuitively suspects that the cave has some nasty surprises in store for him. So most youngsters won't expose themselves to this kind of internal exploration unless accompanied by an adult who they feel is in tune with and understands their mood. This attunement creates a sense of security because it assures the boy or girl that, if anything truly disturbing does turn up inside the cave, the adult and his understanding will be there to provide immediate support and reassurance. And one effect of a reflection like "You sound anxious" or "You sound worried" is that it tells the boy or girl, "You have an understanding, attuned dad right here."

Another important effect is that it also encourages a youngster to begin asking herself why she feels the emotion described in Dad's reflection. And sooner or later, the five-, ten-, or fifteen-year-old who has begun asking herself, "Why do I feel angry?" or "Why do I feel upset?" will arrive at the part of the particular cave she's exploring where all the hidden messages are written.

To illustrate why, I'm going to put Billy Phelan in front of the cave marked "Seth" and show how a few thoughtful reflections would make him begin asking the kinds of questions that would get him inside it, and in front of the wall where the message "Seth intimidates me" is written.

The reason I said the best initial reflection for Billy's dad would be "Gee, you didn't sound very relaxed the other night" is that sometimes the emotions hidden messages produce are experienced as a vague global unpleasantness. So this initial reflection would make Billy ask himself, "Why didn't I feel relaxed the other night?" and once he answered it by saying, "I know why; I was anxious," he'd be inside the cave.

Children usually will tell you the thoughts your reflections produce. So when Billy replied, "I guess I was anxious, Dad," I'd offer a reflection that would encourage him to look at why he was anxious, like "So, something must have been bothering you the other night." This would have the effect of putting him in the part of Seth's cave where the troubling messages are kept, because once Billy started thinking about why he was anxious, his father and New Age music would be quickly eliminated as suspects.

Billy's next reply, "I guess Seth was making me nervous," would produce my third—and, I suspect, last—reflection. Since hearing me say, "You think Seth makes you anxious," would make Billy say to himself, "Yes, I do. I wonder why?" and the eyes of the child who's asking himself that question are about to fall on the message "Seth intimidates me."

As I pointed out earlier, hidden messages are often interconnected in ways that will carry a child in new and unexpected directions. So Billy's discoveries about Seth might turn out to be only a springboard. From Seth he might move to another problematic friend who, since he's also Billy's lab partner, might in turn lead Billy to the cave marked "Mr. Giodarno," his science teacher.

You can actually see these kinds of unexpected connections being made by Nicholas Halsey, the boy in the transcript which follows.

Within a few sentences Nicholas, who was taped for a project study, identifies his first hidden message—teachers are bossy—but as you'll also see, this discovery is only the starting point for a conversation which, thanks to his dad, Gardner's, skillful reflecting, produces a series of increasingly unexpected, painful, and important revelations.

The emotions being reflected are italicized. The transcript reads:

> Son: I wish I were a grownup so I could do anything I wanted.
> Father: You think life's *unfair*.
> Son: Yeah, grownups get to stay out late and do lots of other things. Someone's always telling kids what to do.

Father: You feel grownups are always pushing kids around.

Son: Well, no, Dad, not all grownups. Mostly I'm talking about teachers.

Father: You *feel* teachers are too bossy.

Son: Yeah, especially teachers. A teacher can make you do anything he wants. I hate that.

Father: You *don't like* the authority your teachers have over you?

Son: It's more than not like, Dad, I hate it. I hate the homework assignments teachers give out, the way they can make you stay after school, and get you kicked off the baseball team if your grades aren't good.

Father: So you really *hate* everything about your teachers.

Son: Well actually, Dad, some of my teachers are okay. It's Mr. O'Connor, my homeroom teacher, who I can't stand. I'm stuck with him until June.

Father: And that *upsets* you because you feel trapped.

Son: Yeah, he has this bunch of kids who are his teacher's pets. He lets them do anything. The rest of us, boy, if we're late with a homework assignment or getting to class, he has a fit and makes us stay after school.

Father: And that makes you *angry*.

Son: Yeah, especially since all these teacher's pets are so popular with the rest of the kids. They all have millions of friends.

Father: You *wonder* what makes them so popular, Nick?

Son: Yeah, in a way I do, Dad. Because I don't really have many friends at school.

Father: You're not as popular as *you'd like* to be, Nick?

Son: Yeah, I mean it would be nice to have everyone say hello to you. That's what happens when one of Mr. O'Connor's pets walks down the hall. Everyone practically falls over themselves saying "Hi."

Father: You *wish* the other kids treated you that way, son.

Son: The thing is, Dad, to be treated that way all the other kids have to think you're neat.

Father: And you *worry,* Nick, that that's not the way you're thought of.

Son: Yeah, Dad, I do. Actually, sometimes, some of the other kids make jokes about me being a nerd.

One of the impressive things about Gardner Halsey's behavior in this conversation is his willingness to hang back and let Nick make his own discoveries. Gardner was well aware of Nick's peer problems and had been for some time. But he knew he couldn't solve those problems, and he knew Nick couldn't either, until he first stopped blocking them and, instead, admitted them to himself.

So in his talk, Gardner did what all skillful users of reflection do: he used the technique to put an umbrella of paternal understanding over his son's head and to guide him inside the cave, but then he stepped aside and let Nick make his own discoveries. The technical name for this role is facilitator, and it is not only the most appropriate role for a listening dad but also for a reflecting one.

Now, let's see what you've learned about reflection from Gardner. Imagine, for a moment, that you're John Uterhof and your daughter, Margery, has just replied to your cheery hello by offering you one of the Oreos from the double pack in her lap and by saying, "Gee, Dad, I wish Timmy would call; there are a few things I'd like to say to him."

Which of the following four statements would best reflect her remark?

1. Be patient, hon. I have a feeling Tim will call.
2. You sound upset; let's have a talk about Timmy now.
3. You're upset because Timmy isn't calling you, aren't you?
4. Things change. A few months from now, you and Tim may find a way to work out your problems.

Perfect Dad will tell you to pick replies 1 and 4, but having become an expert on his tactics, you reject his choices because you know they both provide the kind of false reassurances that break the circle of father-child understanding. Reply 2, however, tempts you. It accurately reflects the feelings in Margery's statement (upset) and it gets to the point quickly (let's talk). But it also has a fundamental drawback. It rushes the point, and a child with a hidden message, especially a threatening or painful hidden message (like guilt about a boyfriend), isn't in a mood to be rushed. She'll want to be given the freedom to approach her message in her way and at her pace. And the only one of the choices that gives her this kind of latitude is reply 3: "You're upset because Timmy isn't calling you, aren't you?" This reflection acknowledges Margery's feelings, but it is also open-ended enough to allow her to circle around her hidden message a few times and then come at it in her own way and in her own time.

Now let's imagine that you're Sam Aberjanassi, and you've just arrived home from the second meeting. On walking into the living room, you see a contrite-looking Ricky, who says to you, "Dad, I was a rat for knocking Tommy off his bike the other day."

Which of these statements best reflects Ricky's feelings?

1. I've been thinking about Tommy, too, Rick, and I think you should feel bad about what happened.
2. You feel so bad, you feel like a rat for hurting Tommy.
3. I'm glad you're thinking about Tommy. You did a terrible thing to him.

This list of choices will stump most dads. Numbers 1 and 3 are clearly too critical, and neither reflects the emotion in Ricky's admission. Number 2, on the other hand, does reflect it. So it's the correct answer. But since it also contains a word that most fathers don't like ("rat"), most fathers would be reluctant to use it. No man wants to hear his child call himself a rat, just as no man wants to hear his youngster use words like "hate." But ugly-sounding as such words are, they represent how the child feels. And if you insert your own attitudes into the reflection process by correcting him (as in "Don't use words like that"), you not only tell him, "I don't respect your right to feel the way you do," you risk disrupting the process.

This almost happens to Gardner at one point in the transcript. He tries to soften one of Nick's harsher statements by amending it to "You don't like your teachers," and Nick replies by restating his original remark: "I hate my teachers." This was his way of asking his dad, "Are you still with me?" And if Gardner hadn't quickly corrected himself and said, "So you hate your teachers," their conversation would have ended right there.

This time imagine you're George Phelan. And a very sheepish-looking Billy has just said to you, "Dad, I feel kind of bad about the other night. But I always feel funny when Seth talks about what a great football player he is." Which reply best reflects the emotion underneath this statement?

1. Is that an apology I hear?
2. You sound like you're upset about the other night.
3. I still feel funny about the other night, too, Billy. I wish you wouldn't behave like that, especially in front of one of your friends.
4. I understand, son. You feel bad. But Seth must have some arm. He said he completed four for four passes in his last game.

Answers 2 and 4 are both accurate reflections of the emotion underneath Billy's words. But 4 contains a trap many reflecting dads fall into. If the content of the child's message is especially interesting, at a certain point he'll stop reflecting feelings and start talking about that content—as in "Seth must have some arm." Often you have to pick up on the things a child says to keep the reflection process moving. At several points in the transcript, for example, Gardner refers to teachers and friends Billy's mentioned. But if you begin to focus solely or even just largely on content, you'll derail the process. Which is why, in this case, the appropriate response to Billy would be 2: "You sound like you're upset about the other night."

Happily, the dads in the fall group also learned a great deal from Gardner. (I had handed out transcripts of his conversation with Nick to each one.) In the two role plays which ended the second session, all the reflecting missteps I've just described were avoided.

The subject of the first role play was a post-Seth conversation between George and Billy Phelan. The participants were George, who played himself, and Roger Levine, who played Billy, and the springboard for their conversation was Billy/Roger's observation, "Seth's a neat kid, isn't he?"

Father: Yes, your friend Seth's a nice boy.
Son: Isn't he terrific? All the kids like him, including me.
Father: Everyone wants to be Seth's friend.
Son: Yeah, Dad, Seth's the coolest guy in our school.
Father: You really think a lot of Seth, don't you, Billy?
Son: I hope he had a good time, Dad. I can never tell with Seth.
Father: You sound a little worried about Seth.
Son: Seth's kinda hard to predict, Dad. Sometimes he's nice to me; other times he ignores me.
Father: Seth never lets you know where you stand with him? That can be upsetting, Billy.
Son: Yeah, Dad, it sure can be.

Father: It sounds like you're concerned about Seth's opinion.

Son: I want him to think I'm as neat as he is and I'm not sure he does. He kinda intimidates me.

The session's second role play was built around John and Margery Uterhof. I asked John, who played himself, to imagine that he had just walked in the door and found Margery, who was played by Dave Pullio, sitting on her bed eating a bag of potato chips.

Father: What are you watching, dear?

Daughter: "Hollywood Squares," Dad.

Father: May I have one of your potato chips, Margery?

Daughter: Sure, Dad, take two.

Father: You don't seem very involved in your program, dear.

Daughter: Ah, it's okay, Dad.

Father: Are you preoccupied?

Daughter: Sort of.

Father: I know it's hard to concentrate when you're upset.

Daughter: It's all that Timmy's fault.

Father: You're still angry with him, aren't you, dear?

Daughter: I hate him.

Father: You hate Timmy?

Daughter: Yeah, I hate him, I hate him.

Father: He must have hurt you badly.

Daughter: He did. Timmy's a retard.

> Father: You're very upset about Timmy, aren't
> you, dear?
> Daughter: Yeah, Dad. Can we talk about it?

Those last five words are the magic words every reflection process should produce. And if you don't hear
them within a few minutes, or if your child suddenly seems
puzzled or uninterested in your reflections, chances are
you've misidentified his emotion. In such a case, the best
thing to do is backtrack and ask him directly, "How are
you feeling?" Then, once he's told you, offer him a reflection which restates his feelings.

Of course, your boy or girl won't be so considerate
about your hidden messages—and dads have them, too.
You'll have to rely on your own skills to deal with them.
And the purpose of the next chapter is to provide you
with those skills. We're going to look at the nature of
paternal hidden messages, why they are such a common
phenomenon, how to identify them, and what to do about
them.

B: Self-Directed Skills

The skills in group one are designed to help you identify and express your own thoughts and feelings. The two skills in this category are:

1. Self-awareness
2. Self-expression

3

Four Reasons Why Kids Don't Talk to Dads

*D*ave Pullio: A Fantasy. Around noon on the Saturday morning between the third and the fourth sessions, Dave Pullio was sitting at his kitchen table when he felt the gentle tap of a finger on his shoulder and turned around to find Dwight Evans, the Boston Red Sox's right fielder, standing behind him with an unhappy look on his face and a Red Sox cap in his hands. Mr. Evans apologized for the intrusion, but said, "Dave, I have a problem. I only hit .220 last year, and if I only hit .220 this year, I won't have a next year with the Sox. What do you think I should do about my swing?"

Dave was flattered and touched that, in a moment of career crisis, one of his biggest heroes, Mr. Evans, chose to turn to him for help and guidance. But, in truth, Dave also found the right fielder's presence in his kitchen at this particular moment distracting. He was in the middle of a conversation with his daughter, Keri, which had begun a few minutes earlier when Keri sat down at the table beside him and said, "Daddy, Gina and I had a humongous fight last night about who's more popular, me or her."

The unmistakable undercurrent of anger in Keri's words had produced the paternal reflection "You sound real mad this morning, Pumpkin." And when Keri replied by saying, "I am. Tubby made fun of my hair last night," Dave offered a series of reflections which led Keri from Gina, to Maria Plassio, Gina's mother, to Anthony Plassio, her older brother, to Anthony's best friend, Vinnie Orsini, whose cave Dave and Keri were standing outside of when the unhappy-looking Mr. Evans arrived in the Pullio kitchen with his hat in his hand, his .220 batting average, and his problem, and gently tapped Dave on the shoulder.

At first Dave was polite but firm with the beseeching but distracting right fielder. "Dwight," he said, "I'd love to talk to you about your swing, I really would. I'm worried about that .220, too. But now's not a good time. I got my daughter, here. You understand."

Mr. Evans nodded and said he understood, but he looked disappointed.

"Daddy, Daddy, c'mon, c'mon," Keri said, grabbing Dave's hand. "Let's go."

"Relax, Pumpkin, relax. Where's the fire?"

"Daddy, I want to take you inside Vinnie's cave and show you where all my secret feelings for him are written."

Buzzzzzzzzzz.

"Ouch!" That hurt. But where did the buzz come from? Dave looked around. Out of nowhere, it seemed, strange.

"Daddy, you're going to let me show you my feelings for Vinnie, aren't you?"

"Sure, Pumpkin, sure. How many feelings for Vinnie do you want to show me?"

"All of them, Daddy."

"All of them?"

"Uh-huh, all of them."

Buzzzzzzzzzzzzzzzzzzzzzzzzzzzzzzz."OUCH!" This time the buzz was so bad, if the quick-witted Mr. Evans hadn't caught him first, Dave would've fallen off his chair. "You're all right, aren't you, Dave? You almost took a bad fall."

The right fielder looked concerned, even solicitous; and it was nice in Dwight's arms, and hey, when he talked—"Dwight, say something to me."

"Dave, I hit .320 my last year of triple-A ball."

No buzz. Better double-check. "Say something else, Dwight."

"Dave, if you were the Red Sox's manager, I'd hit .320 next year and we'd end the season in first place, not second, like this year."

No, definitely no buzz. And Dwight was smart, besides.

"Pumpkin," Dave said, "why don't you go ahead inside Vinnie's cave? Maybe I'll meet you later, after lunch." Then, turning to the Red Sox right fielder, he said, "Dwight, the first thing you have to do about your swing is . . ."

"So you never got inside Mr. Orsini's cave," I said, after Dave finished telling his story to the group.

Dave shook his head. "Nope, I just got to the front door. Strange thing is, until we got there, I was all ears. Keri's a funny kid; she did a terrific imitation of Tony Plassio Saturday. But as soon as she started talking about Vinnie, I began hearing these strange noises."

"Like a buzz, Dave?"

"Yeah, sort of, and, then, the next thing I knew, I was giving Dwight Evans batting lessons."

The real culprit in Dave's story will, I think, surprise you. It wasn't Dwight Evans, or even that annoying buzz he kept hearing, but rather the emotional unawareness he—and so many other men—suffer from. Keri's disclosures were embarrassing and disconcerting to him, but as an inexperienced emotion-spotter, Dave didn't realize that. So his unidentified embarrassment and discomfiture did what all unidentified feelings do, they slipped underground and began producing a buzz. Sometimes, like Dave, the man hears the buzz itself; other times, he only notices its signals, like feeling antsy and vaguely uncomfortable. But, in all cases, the outcome is the same: if the feeling producing the buzz isn't recognized—and it usually isn't if the victim is a man—the buzz grows until, finally, it gets so big and annoying, it has to be dealt with. And one of the ways—one of the more benign ways—a man deals with it is by doing what Dave did: he tries to take his mind off it by thinking of something else, like Dwight Evans.

There's no known antidote for the source of the buzz—paternal feelings. Part of being a listening, caring parent is opening up and exposing yourself to things that occasionally do embarrass, discomfit, or even hurt or sadden you. But there is a remedy for the buzz itself and for all the attendant problems it creates. This chapter's skill, *Self-awareness,* is a very effective one, because it strikes directly at the source of the buzz by showing a man how to identify the nameless emotions that cause it.

Giving a name to a feeling brings it into awareness, and that strikes directly at the buzz, because once its source is up in the light, it automatically stops. Only unidentified feelings produce buzzes. Of course, if the feeling is unpleasant, like embarrassment or sadness, you still have to deal with it. But identification can help a listening dad here, too. If you are sensitive to your emotions, you can manage them in a way that removes some of the sting. Take Dave's case.

Knowing what he felt would have let him remind himself that the parents of fifteen-year-olds often do hear embarrassing or troubling things from their kids. In other words, it would have let him put his emotions into the kind of perspective that would have made them easier for him to bear and, hence, made them less likely to disrupt his ability to continue listening to Keri.

The reason dads rarely get to the point in conversations where they can begin making management decisions about their feelings is that men aren't socialized or encouraged to be emotionally aware. So, more often than not, their feelings remain unidentified, and, more often than not, the upshot is that the buzz from those feelings grows and grows until finally it shapes itself into one of four distinct paternal syndromes, all of which to varying degrees break the circle of father-child understanding.

Dave's reaction is an example of the first and most benign of these syndromes, *Distraction*. At the project, we see a lot of this particular syndrome among first-time skill users. As the dad masters the program's first two skills, he begins hearing his youngster in a new and different way, and that, in turn, begins producing some new, troubling, and hard-to-manage feelings in him.

This phenomenon is so common among our newer dads, in fact, that I wasn't surprised that early in the session on Self-awareness, George Phelan also reported he had fallen victim to it. In George's case, though, the buzz was produced by an unidentified paternal sadness. A few days earlier, Seth and a group of his friends had surrounded

Billy Phelan in the school cafeteria and made fun of his new suede jacket.

"That night at dinner when Billy told me what had happened, I was so mad I was going to call Seth's father," George said. "But afterwards, when I went into Billy's room to get all of the gruesome details—*bang*—my American Express bill popped into my mind and I got so distracted thinking about it, I started falling back on generic replies instead of listening. Perfect Dad would've loved me. I even said, 'Well, I like your jacket, Billy.' One paternal emotion I didn't have any trouble identifying the other night was guilt."

Such paternal guilt is a complicating factor in many cases of the buzz-related syndromes. Mike Danzig, a former program dad, is a case in point. Mike fell victim to the second of these syndromes, which we call *The Rubber Band*. Instead of trying to cope with the buzz through distractions, its victims let the buzz build and build until, finally, like a rubber band stretched to its limit then released, they *snap* and pour out all their unidentified anger or hurt or pain into a thunderous explosion like the one that sent Mike flying off his couch one night and landed him in my office a week later with a very bad case of paternal guilt.

Mike told me his sudden fiery levitation had so frightened his six-year-old, Davy, that Davy fled the Danzig living room in terror and tears. And as of Mike's visit to me, which was nine days later, Davy still was so wary of his volcanic father that he refused to be left alone in a room with him. "If I walk in and there's no one else around," Mike said, "Davy'll make a polite excuse, then get up and go look for my wife, Janice. I really feel ashamed of myself."

Mike's guilt was compounded by the fact that his eruption—as Rubber Band eruptions often are—was triggered by a very trivial and innocent event. Davy had wanted the pillows of the sofa Mike was sitting on to build a Thundertank, which happens to be the favorite weapon of Davy's favorite TV heroes, the Thundercats. And being like most men—an obliging father—Mike had said, "Sure, Davy, take them," but also being, like most men, emotionally unaware, Mike failed to ask a question that a more aware parent would have asked.

The question was "Why can't I sit still on the sofa?" and it became urgently relevant about ten minutes into Mike's sojourn on the pillowless sofa, since by this time, he was bouncing around on it like a Mexican jumping bean. This paternal antsyness was being produced by a buzz of unidentified anger that had had enough time to build a terrific head of steam. Mike was furious at having to endure the hardships and discomforts of a pillowless couch in the name of a Thundertank. But because he did not know he was angry and was not the easily distracted type, Mike's anger grew and grew until, finally, it rolled itself up into a tremendous fireball and detonated in Davy's face, which so disturbed little Davy, it was nearly three months before his relationship with his dad was restored to its preexplosion intimate trust.

Robert Reddiger's alienation from his father, Harold, was even more deep-seated. And if you'd met the Harold Reddiger who walked into my office two years ago, you'd understand why. Harold was the *Tin Man Syndrome* incarnate.

Of the four strategies men adopt to cope with the buzz of unidentified feelings, in many ways, the Tin Man's is the simplest and most direct. Instead of trying to divert himself from the buzz with distractions, or rolling it up into a hand grenade and tossing it at someone, the Tin Man takes it and the feelings producing it, puts them in a closet, locks the door, and throws away the key. And because Tin Men have a lot of self-control, they're usually able to keep these emotions in the closet. But when you lock up your feelings by denying them, inevitably you also lock up a part of your heart and soul. And when you do that, you begin to lose the ability to feel, and as that capacity drains out of you, you become like those windup dolls five-and-ten-cent stores sell—mechanical and rigid.

The Tin Man Syndrome is a very difficult one for children—who thrive on parental emotion—to handle. And over the years, in a thousand different ways, Robert Reddiger had told his dad this. In big and small, subtle and unsubtle ways, Robert had kept saying, "Dad, I need some warmth, some tenderness, some sadness, some *life* from you." And over the years, in a thousand big and little, subtle and unsubtle ways, Harold Reddiger had found ways to rationalize the look of hurt and disappointment he always saw on his son's face when he said, "No, Robert, I won't give you any of those things." But the night Robert's Little League team lost an important playoff game, Harold finally ran out of rationalizations.

At dinner, Robert, who was very disappointed by the loss, violated a key Tin Man tenet—never show feeling— by breaking into tears when he began talking about the game, which so annoyed his father that Harold turned to him and said, "For God's sakes, Bobby, stop crying like a baby. It was only a baseball game." To his credit, when Bobby shouted back, "You don't care about me, Dad, do you? You never have," Harold finally stopped ducking. This time, he recognized his son's words for what they were, a sign of deep alienation, and two weeks later Harold was in my office asking for help.

There's a nice postscript to the Reddigers' story. It takes the form of a picture I came across in the sports pages of *The Boston Globe* last year, when Robert's team won the Eastern Massachusetts Little League Playoffs. It shows former Tin Man Harold hugging his very happy son in full view of hundreds of fans. Occasionally, we all need reminders of why we do what we do. Harold and Robert's picture, which now hangs in a frame in my office, serves as my reminder.

Of the four syndromes, it is my educated guess that the Tin Man is the least common, the Rubber Band is the second least common, Distraction the most common, and the Mixed Messenger, the last of the buzz-related syndromes, the second most common.

Typically, the Mixed Messenger deals with the buzz of unidentified feeling by letting it ooze out in his body language, voice tone, facial expressions, and movement. But since even in the face of great calamity, a victim of this syndrome keeps his words calm, reasonable, even friendly, inevitably a discrepancy arises between those words—which represent what the victim thinks he's feeling—and his deeds—which represent what he's really feeling—that send mixed messages to his boy or girl.

It is also my educated guess that with the rise of the New Father, the incidence of this particular syndrome is on the upswing. Today, most men want to be seen as a friend, a companion, and a helpmate to their children. So when one of those children does something disturbing, like accidentally knocking a freshly cleaned pair of pants on the floor with a Captain Power Death Ray, the New

Father tries to respond to this mishap the way he thinks a New Father should: calmly, reasonably—like a friend. But since it is annoying to have Captain Power's Death Ray add your freshly cleaned pants to its body count, inevitably the New Father will get angry. But since he'll also try to deny that anger, it will end up slipping out in his voice tone, body language, and general demeanor, all of which will combine to tell the owner of the Captain Power Death Ray, "If you don't get rid of that thing now, I'm going to brain you."

At first the discrepancy between the Mixed Messenger's words and deeds confuses a child. But if the discrepancy continues for any length of time, eventually the child's confusion vanishes. After one or two years of hearing Dad's words say "I feel A" while seeing Dad's behavior say "I feel B," the child concludes the problem isn't his confusion, but Dad's deviousness—he never tells you what he really feels.

A role play George Phelan and I did during the session on Self-awareness illustrates how unidentified emotions can make a man vulnerable to the Mixed Messenger and other syndromes. Our role play didn't last long enough to produce the kind of big buzzes which could have turned George into a windup doll or cannonball. But the transcript of it, which follows, is worth examining closely, because within it are three unidentified emotions that if left unidentified would have pointed George in their general direction.

As you read it through, see if you can identify the three feelings that slipped unnoticed past George as he tried, not very successfully, to get Billy (who was played by me) to pick up his room.

> Father: Billy, your room looks like Hogan's Alley. Please, pick it up.
>
> Child: But Dad, I'm watching "Pee Wee's Playhouse"; I don't want to miss any of it.
>
> Father [sighing]: Billy, why don't you ever listen to me? Please, I've asked you to pick up your room.
>
> Child: Dad, I'll pick it up when the commercial's on, I promise. Cross my heart and hope to die.
>
> Father: I'll bet your friends don't give their dads a big song and dance when they're told to pick up.

[At this point, I told George to imagine we'd arrived at the commercial break.]

> Father: Okay, Billy, the commercial's on. You promised; pick up now.
>
> Child: I have to go to the bathroom.
>
> Father: Oh, God, I don't believe you; all right, but make it quick, please.
>
> Child: [returning from the bathroom]: Oh look, Pee Wee's back on. I'll clean up after his show's over.
>
> Father: I'll tell you what. Pick up your room now and I'll take you to McDonald's for lunch.
>
> Child: I can't. I've got a ballgame later. C'mon, Dad, let me watch the rest of Pee Wee.
>
> Father: Billy, I'm going to shut the TV off if you don't start picking up.
>
> Child: Dad, don't do that. I love Pee Wee.
>
> Father: My heart is stone. The TV is off.

Child: Aw, you're a rat, Dad.
Father: C'mon mister, be quiet and pick up.

Did you notice the paternal sigh that preceded the remark "Billy, why don't you ever listen to me?" That signaled George's first unidentified emotion: helplessness. Getting Billy to obey him without yelling or standing there and monitoring Billy's behavior had always been a problem for George. But he didn't realize how helpless this disregard of his paternal authority made him feel until he saw himself on the videotape I'd made of our role play. Hearing himself sigh and seeing the Oh-God-What-Do-I-Do-Now look on his face as I handed him excuse after excuse, George shook his head and said, "I look like a pretty forlorn character, don't I?"

His second unidentified emotion emerged a few minutes later and it was signaled by the words "Oh, God, I don't believe you." George agreed that this was the declaration of a frustrated father and when he saw himself uttering it on the tape, he amended his description of this declaration by inserting the adverb "unknowingly" in front of "frustrated."

George's last unidentified emotion emerged near the end of the role play when, as Billy, I told him, "I can't. I've got a ballgame later." George didn't remember having any particular reaction to my words. But when he saw the way my rejection of his luncheon invitation made his shoulders sag on the tape, he agreed my "no" had produced an unidentified paternal sadness. The goal of *Learn to Identify Your Feelings,* the first step in Self-awareness, is to give a man a handle on feelings like George's before they get big enough to cause problems. There are two ways to do this. One is by tuning in and actually listening to your feelings.

A lot of fathers who get buzzed wouldn't if they took the time to do what mothers often do: tune in and listen to their own feelings. When we get to Self-awareness's second step, I'll show you how to facilitate this listening, but for the most part, it doesn't involve any special technique or magical procedure, just a willingness to stop and ask yourself, "What am I feeling?" when you're tickled by an emotion, instead of doing what most men do—trying to push it away.

I should point out that, given his inexperience, even the dad who's trying to listen will, at first, have trouble putting concrete names like sadness, anger, hurt, or warmth on what he hears; many times he may even find it hard to hear the buzz these feelings produce. But what he'll always notice are the signals their buzz throws off. And since, in a general way, different buzzes produce different signals, taking note of these signals will give you a second way to identify your feelings.

The stories we've looked at in this chapter, for example, would serve as a good introduction to the signals thrown off by the buzz of unpleasant paternal emotions like anger, pain, annoyance, hurt, or embarrassment. Think, for example, of Mike Danzig's antsyness or the distractions that visited George Phelan and Dave Pullio this week.

Difficulty concentrating; overreaction to simple, inconsequential things; a vague, global feeling of discomfort akin to the one you have in the doctor's office; and even a sudden case of the munchies are other telltale signals of the buzz produced by upsetting or unhappy paternal feelings.

Warmth, tenderness, love, and other happier paternal feelings also produce a characteristic buzz: ease of touch, unusual spontaneity, enjoyment, and tranquillity being some of the common signals. The dad who suddenly finds himself able to do what he and most men usually can't do comfortably—hold, hug, or otherwise physically touch his child—or the dad who finds himself talking with an unaccustomed freedom and volubility, or liking a game he normally doesn't like, such as "Operation" or "Fireball Island," or who, on this particular night, really doesn't mind that Captain Power's Death Ray has just added his pants to its body count, is a dad in the throes of a happy unidentified feeling.

The goal of *Emotional Record Keeping,* Self-awareness's second step, is to help a man get a handle on these buzzes, and on his emotions generally; and it involves using a notebook to keep a written record of the emotions and buzzes you note during father-child interactions and the words or events that seem to produce them. I know diary keeping involves an extra effort, but keeping a written record for three or four weeks of what you felt and when and under what circumstances you felt it will give you what you can't get when you keep track in your head: a clear look at your parental emotional patterns. And once you have that, you'll be able to use your feelings to enhance and strengthen the circle of father-child understanding.

Exhibit A, or how record keeping serves this important cause, is Mike Danzig, whose log finally let him start managing the feelings that had made them and him a source of fear and intimidation for six-year-old Davy Danzig. In Mike's case the discovery that brought about this happy change emerged two weeks into his record keeping, and it centered on something he noticed about the unhappy buzz that always preceded his explosions. Mike had always thought of himself as hair-triggered, but as he traced the trajectory of this mean little buzz, he found it and the anger it signaled actually built slowly, passing through four distinct stages, each with its own markers, and this information gave him a kind of Early Warning System. He now knew that Stage One of the buzz, inability to focus, signaled an incipient paternal annoyance. Which meant, if he took action as soon as he noticed it, either by asking Davy to stop doing what he found irritating or by getting up and leaving the room, he could prevent the buzz from proceeding to Stage Two, antsyness; Stage Three, teeth-grinding; and Stage Four, eruption.

Exhibit B of how record keeping can help a man to use paternal emotions to strengthen the circle of parent-child understanding is Harold Reddiger and his son, Robert. The day Harold began his log I pointed out to him what I pointed out to you a few pages ago: moments of free and easy paternal conversation are a sign of unidentified happy or warm or tender paternal feeling. And since these were the feelings Harold—and Robert—needed most, I told him to take special note of them in his log, which Harold, being Harold, did with painstaking care. The pattern that arose from these special entries, however, was perplexing at first. It showed paternal conversation to be at its freest and most vocal when Harold and Robert were watching a show like "Nature" or "Wild America" or a "National Geographic" special. And what made the pattern perplexing is that Harold isn't and never has been a wildlife enthusiast. "I don't even watch these shows if Robert isn't around," he told me the night we went over his log. But after we talked for a while, the reason for the pattern became clear.

Harold might not be a wildlife enthusiast, but he did enjoy explaining and describing—being an educator, really—and these shows brought out this side of him. As he and Robert watched elephants trampling across African plains or jaguars treading through Amazon jungles, Harold could dip into his limited store of zoological knowledge or fairly extensive store of geographical knowledge and explain some special characteristic of the animal or locale featured on the show they were watching. And these paternal explanations and descriptions were greeted with such enthusiasm that the night we went over his log, Harold told me he thought he had a budding zoologist on his hands. I'll tell you something I didn't tell Harold; I don't think Robert Reddiger is any more interested in zoology than the man in the moon. But like all ten-year-olds, he likes being with an interesting, informative, outgoing, and warm father; and that's the kind of father Harold became when he had an opportunity to play educator. And now that his log had identified the kinds of activities that brought out this side of Harold, I suggested similar father-son activities, like visits to Bunker Hill and the U.S.S. *Constitution,* which would bring out more of it. It was a small start, but, as the picture on my wall shows, a good one.

Harold's and Mike's stories illustrate what a man can learn when he follows the three rules of Emotional Record Keeping:

- Record the buzzes you feel, when you first start to feel them and what factors seem to trigger them and why.
- Ditto the emotions you're able to identify.
- Pay special attention to situations, events, and statements that produce especially strong reactions.

The week's worth of entries each member brought to the group's next meeting reflected how carefully everyone had been in following these rules. But they also reflected something else. And it shows up in the list of paternal emotions I wrote on the blackboard as each dad read from his notebook. By the time the last person had spoken, my list looked like this:

Anger (five members)
Irritation (four members)
Frustration (four members)
Resentment (three members)
Hostility (four members)
Aggression (three members)
Warmth (one member)

Though this list doesn't represent the six warm, funny, compassionate, tender, sweet men I'd come to know, it's a very good representation of the force that had shaped them all—the male socialization process.

I don't want to be unduly harsh to this process. God knows it already has more than enough accusing fingers pointed at it these days, some of them unfairly, since it has to have gotten a couple of big things right to have produced these six men and a lot of the other men I know. But I'm afraid when it comes to feelings, it does let a man— and, usually, everyone in his life—down, because it says there are only certain emotions you can feel and still be appropriately masculine. So when men do start paying attention to their feelings, these are the ones they hear most clearly—and most comfortably.

Anger, hostility, aggression—the list I compiled on the blackboard is a pretty good representative sample of process-approved emotions. But since two thirds of life involves process-disapproved ones like sadness, hurt, love, joy, tenderness, pain, and disappointment, the process's bias puts a man in the unhappy position of spending two thirds of his life either being embarrassed by what he feels or trying to hide it under a rug, and that hurts his child and it hurts him.

The child suffers because, being comfortable only with process-approved emotions, her dad remembers only the things the child does that make Dad angry or annoyed or irritable and not the things that make Dad feel tender and warm. And then Dad suffers because he doesn't get any of the validation and warmth that come with remembering his youngster's thoughtfulness and sweetness, and because thirty years from now, sitting in his rocking chair, he is not going to have many good memories to warm him in his old age.

I'm afraid I don't have any magical solutions to the problem of process-disapproved emotions, except to say, "Don't be afraid of them." There's nothing unmanly about being sad or hurt or tender or warm. These are the feelings that give life depth and richness, and give each of us a little light that shines.

Once you acknowledge them, I think you'll be surprised at how many of these feelings you have and how easily they flow out of you. But because they are on the disapproved list, and because men don't have what women do, a tradition of emotional responsivity to consult, occasionally you may get stuck expressing one of them— either because it makes you uncomfortable or because you don't know how to express the feeling in an appropriate way. And here's where Self-awareness can be of some assistance.

It takes the form of *Evoking,* the skill's third step. It's designed to facilitate emotional expression by giving a dad a role model to encourage and guide him. Feelings, especially process-disapproved feelings, flow more easily when you can summon up a memory of a time when your dad—or if not him, your mother or a grandparent—was warm or tender or sad or loving with you or someone you love.

Every man has such memories and evoking them gives him what "Nature" and the U.S.S. *Constitution* gave Harold Reddiger, a way of getting in touch with sides of ourselves that will make better fathers.

A case in point are the three stories that ended the group's discussion of Self-awareness. They were told by Dave Pullio, George Phelan, and Paul Cronin, and their telling came in response to my question: "Does anyone have any memories he could use as a model of emotional expressivity?"

Dave, who spoke first, described an incident that occurred shortly before the death of his father, Angelo.

"Angelo died on September 25, 1978," Dave said. "So around the seventeenth or eighteenth must have been the last time I took him up to Somerville Hospital. By this time he was so sick with cancer, he couldn't even stand; I had to carry him downstairs to my car. I couldn't believe it, my father was a big guy, bigger than me, even, but carrying him down the stairs, it was like carrying Keri. He couldn't have weighed more than a hundred and twenty or a hundred and thirty pounds. Imagine that. Anyway, as I was putting him in the car, he reached up—I had him in my arms like this—he reached up and kissed me. He kissed me on the lips."

Dave paused for a moment.

"I think we all understand how you must have felt, Dave."

"I felt like my life just reached up and kissed me is how I felt, Ron. I know you're talking about memories you can use one time or another. But in a way I use Angelo's memory all the time. It's made a difference with my kids, even with Dominick. Holding, hugging, even kissing him. I don't feel funny about that. Not at all."

George Phelan, who spoke next, began by describing his father.

"First, you have to understand who my father was," he said. "John Phelan was your standard-issue big, beefy Irish cop. He had a face like a lobster, a temper to match, and a beer belly as big as two beach balls. He also thought any man who didn't act like Spencer Tracy belonged in a dress.

"As it turned out, he had—or rather, has—a homosexual son. My older brother Kevin is gay. And one Sunday afternoon when Kevin was twenty and I was seventeen, poor, sweet, brave, stupid Kevin decided to announce his inclination to the Phelan family at dinner. It was like somebody dropped a dead body onto the dinner table. Nobody would look up from their plates because no one wanted to look at the body on the table and no one said anything because no one knew what to say.

"Over the next few days, one by one, my sisters Megan and Mary first, then my mother, then me—actually, it was one of my seventeen-year-old self's finest moments—began circling around Kevin like wagon trains; whatever he was, he was ours first. Not a word was heard from John Phelan, Boston Police Department, though. He wouldn't talk to Kevin and he wouldn't talk about Kevin—to my mother or to my sisters or to me. He'd just come home every night with his *Boston Record,* open a bottle of Ballantine ale, and sit in his big, old, ugly green chair in the parlor reading and nursing his ale. For a couple of weeks, it was like living with a thermonuclear device. 'Oh, God,' everyone kept thinking, 'when's he going to go off?'

"You know what? He never did. One Saturday three weeks later, one very hot Saturday—I remember because I was leaning out my bedroom window for some air—I heard the screen door on the back porch bang and then the crunch of footsteps coming down the back-porch stairs. My window was right over the porch but there was a little roof on it, so I had to lean way out to see who was down there. The first thing I saw coming out from under the roof was a hand carrying a glass of lemonade, then a beer belly, then the bald spot on the top of my father's head. He walked over to Kevin, who was sitting under a tree reading, bent down, and handed him the lemonade. Nothing was said, but Kevin knew what he was being told and so did I; so would anyone who knew John Phelan. It was all very simple, but it said everything that had to be said."

George smiled.

"It was the way Spencer Tracy would have done it. And it taught me to be brave enough emotionally to love my kids, whatever choices they make for themselves."

"That's the best kind of emotional memory a father can leave his son," I said.

Paul Cronin, who'd had a very difficult and painful relationship with his father, followed a suggestion I'd made earlier and used a tender memory of his mother to evoke some important, but process-disapproved, emotions.

"My story's about the Christmas of—let's see, I was ten, so it's about the Christmas of 1958," Paul said. "I loved model planes and ships as a kid. So two days before

Christmas, my mother took me to Levy's, a hobby shop in Union Square—I think it's still there, in fact—to pick out my Christmas presents. I knew we were pretty broke—my father always left us broke—but I figured I had twenty dollars to spend. And I was careful to pick out just under twenty dollars' worth of toys. But when I told my mother I wanted the U.S.S. *Lexington,* a Spitfire, and a Bomber Command Mustang, she shook her head and said, 'I'm sorry, Paul, I only have eight dollars, I can't buy all three; you'll have to pick one.'

"What I remember is the way she put her hand on my shoulder when she said that. I don't want to get mawkish, but her touch was about a lot more than only getting one toy for Christmas. I was an unhappy and—because of the way my father was—a scared little kid. And my mother touched my shoulder in a way that told me she knew how I felt, but she wanted me to know she was there for me now, and she would be there for me as long as I needed her."

"That, in other words, you were safe, Paul?"

Paul thought for a moment.

"Yes, exactly, that I was safe."

The final story of the meeting was told by me. And it was designed to illustrate a phenomenon we call "problem emotions." Every man has a few feelings he finds it especially hard to express, and, generally, these feelings pose a special problem for one of three reasons. Either they make the man feel unmanly or guilty or—as in the case of Phil Dorman, the subject of my story—they trigger unhappy paternal emotions.

Isaac Dorman's directive, authoritarian behavior had left his son with such a pathological fear of sounding directive himself that Phil often was unable to provide paternal guidance even in situations where some paternal guidance was clearly called for. A case in point is the way he reacted to his seventeen-year-old son, Carl's, announcement that he wanted a keg of beer at his high-school graduation party. Phil knew that the presence of the keg would produce more than a few cases of intoxication and that some of those cases would then step into the family car and try to drive home. But even though he was aware of this danger Phil couldn't shake his fear of sounding authoritarian. A limp "Well, I don't know if that's such a good idea" was the best response he could muster to Carl's announcement about the keg.

What Phil should have said is "I know you and your friends aren't kids anymore. But I think you're all still a few years away from attaining the kind of maturity that allows a person to drink wisely and safely."

This statement is an example of Self-expression. And in the next chapter we're going to look at why this skill allows a dad to express feelings—even ones he normally finds difficult to express—in a way that feels comfortable to him and to his child.

4

How to Say No (Nicely)

My secretary, whose name is Greta and who looks a bit like Brünnhilde, has one of those steely temperaments that don't surrender easily to panic. So the Friday afternoon she announced I had a call on line three, and it sounded like an emergency, my heart leapt to my throat. If Greta was alarmed, then the apocalypse must be at hand and waiting patiently for me at the other end of line three.

"Ron, hello. Ron. *Ron!!*"

Never was I so happy to hear Sam Aberjanassi's raspy voice. But I could see why Greta had been so alarmed. Sam sounded upset, very upset. And while it took me a few minutes to figure out why he was, even before piecing together all the threads of his very complex tale, I knew I was in the presence of that all-too-common paternal emotion: the fear of saying no.

In Sam's case, the fear was linked—as so many of his parenting experiences seemed to be—to Tommy Logan, who on the way to school a few days earlier had told Ricky that he'd just seen the scariest movie ever, *Jaws*, without being scared once. Sensing that, in some sly way, Tommy was issuing a challenge to his manhood, Ricky had thereupon resolved that he also would see the scariest movie ever without being scared once. So that night he'd said to Sam, "Dad, can we get a video of *Jaws?* Tommy says it's super-scary."

Remembering its star's insatiable appetite, Sam had a good many reservations about this request. There was much in the movie that could frighten Ricky, and nothing that could enlighten or inspire him. But one of the marks of the Fear-of-Saying-No Syndrome is that the desire to please a child often is allowed to outweigh paternal judgment and good sense. So after hesitating for a moment, Sam smiled and said, "Sure, why not, Ricky, I'll pick up a video of it on my way home from work."

Today was Friday and the reason Sam was now sitting in his bathroom with the door shut and the phone cupped to his ear is that all his lightly dismissed reservations had come home to haunt him with a vengeance. As we talked, Ricky was sitting a dozen feet away in the living room vibrating in a state of *Jaws*-induced shock.

"Where are you in the movie now, Sam?" I asked.

I heard the bathroom door creak open.

"Let's see. Oh, God, Ron, it's near the part where the little boy gets eaten. Ricky's going to levitate out of his seat when he sees that."

"He won't let you take the video out?"

"Are you kidding? Why do you think I'm in here with the phone? If he knew I was even thinking about . . . Oh, God, Ron, the little boy just stood up on the beach blanket and waved goodbye to his mother, the poor kid. Ron, he's walking down to the water. Ron, do something, please."

Under other circumstances, I would have told Sam his dilemma was a good example of why a man needs Self-expression, the skill we'd be examining at the next session. But I knew that wouldn't be of any help to him now. So instead, I said: "Look, Sam, it's nearly six o'clock. You'll probably be eating soon."

"Ron!"

"Dinner, Sam. I just mean dinner; tell Ricky it's time for dinner. If he's half as frightened as you say, he'll be happy to be given a graceful exit."

As it turned out, I was right—and not just about Ricky's desire for a graceful exit. I suspected Sam's fear of saying no might be what we at the project call a "problem emotion." These are feelings a father has an especially difficult time expressing. And while they have a number of causes, a leading one is the behavior of the man's own father. If he did something the man particularly disliked, usually the man will bend over backward to avoid repeating that behavior with his child. My guess about Sam was that his dad had been a great nay-sayer, and Sam confirmed it when I ran into him in the hall before the next meeting.

"You're on the mark, Ron," he said. "When I was a kid, I used to think that my dad's three favorite words were 'No, you can't.' "

Ten minutes later, I found myself listening to two other examples of these father-induced problem emotions. The first example came from Dave Pullio, who announced that he'd learned something new about himself the previous Friday night when he realized he'd mistakenly accused Keri of violating her curfew. "I can't admit I made a mistake. Imagine that. My father was the same way. You could catch him red-handed in a mistake, and he'd still stonewall you."

Roger Levine's story was more poignant. For the past three weeks, Roger, who is divorced, had been looking forward to taking his eight-year-old, Max, to the Malden City Club's annual father-son hockey game.

"I must have reminded Max about that game three times," Roger said. "Also, I must have reminded his mother five times, but that's like talking to the wind. I thought I could trust Max to remember, though. So what happens Sunday when I come by to pick him up? I find Max standing on the porch dressed in a blue suit waiting for a ride to a Hanukkah party at the temple.

"You know what he told me when I asked him about our date? 'I forgot, Dad. I forgot.' How can you forget a date with your father? I felt like . . . I didn't feel good."

"Did you tell Max he had hurt you, Roger?"

"No, I didn't. I couldn't bring myself to do it."

"Was your dad one of those macho types who pride themselves on never showing pain or hurt?"

Roger laughed. "No, my father was a nervous little guy like me. Also he was a very good manipulator. Dr. Levine didn't need to shout or threaten because he knew how to use guilt to bully you into obeying him.

"When my sister, Sheila, got accepted at Bennington, for example, he was furious. He hated the idea of Bennington. But instead of telling Sheila, 'Bennington's too bohemian,' he walked around for weeks complaining about how his patients would suffer if he had to spend all his time worrying about a daughter who lived two hundred miles away. And he ended up getting his way. Sheila stayed home and went to Barnard.

"Twenty years from now, I don't want Max telling people how his dad used to manipulate his feelings."

"So what did you tell Max, Rog?"

"I told him, 'Never mind, Maxy, we all make mistakes. We'll do it another time.'"

"I know how Rog feels," Sam said. "If my choice had been to leave *Jaws* on and let Ricky levitate or spend a week feeling guilty for behaving like my father, Ricky would still be levitating. What do you do about problem emotions, Ron?"

Self-expression, the skill we're going to look at in this chapter, is designed to answer Sam's question by giving a man a method of saying the sometimes difficult negative and uncomfortable things a father has to say in a way that won't tap into his painful memories of his dad or into the two other leading sources of paternal problem emotions.

The first is New Father guilt, and its contribution is, I think, easy to understand. A friend isn't supposed to mind an overly loud stereo or yet another request for an advance on next week's allowance, so the New Father's desire to be seen as that friend often leaves him tongue-tied in such situations. Machismo is the other leading cause and, given the way it frowns on feelings like disppointment, sorrow, hurt, and pain, I think its role in problem emotions is equally easy to understand.

What makes Self-expression an effective antidote to all the various causes and sources of problem emotions is that it lets a man state his feelings in a direct, forthright way, but also in a way that, in every situation, says to his boy or girl, "No matter how much we disagree, I understand your thoughts and feelings on this issue and respect them."

To illustrate how it does these two important things, I'm going to put Roger Levine back on Max's front porch. But this time, through literary sleight-of-hand, I'm going to endow Roger with a knowledge of Self-expression and its three steps:

1. Describe your negative feelings rather than blame or accuse.
2. Show an understanding and respect for the child's point of view.
3. Always balance negative remarks with positive ones.

Watch the difference an understanding of these three points makes in Roger's handling of Max:

Child: I'm sorry, Dad, but I can't go to the game with you. I'm going to a Hanukkah party at the temple.

Father: I thought we had made a date for this morning, Max.

Child: I know, I know. But I told you I forgot. Also, I really want to go to this party. All my friends will be there. I don't know any of the kids who'll be at the hockey game.

Father: I understand being with your friends is important to you, Max. But I'm really disappointed that you aren't coming to the game. I've told all the guys what a terrific son I have. They were really looking forward to meeting you this morning.

Child: I'm sorry, Dad, honest. But Rabbi Goldstein said he was looking forward to seeing me at the party. Also, I don't want to disappoint him.

Father: I know you care about Rabbi Goldstein. And I know you care about me, too, and I think you have a pretty good idea of how much you mean to me. So I think it's important for you to know that I feel hurt that you forgot our date. Okay, son?

Child: Okay. And Dad . . .

Father: Yes?

Child: Thank you.

One reason for that unexpected "thank you" of Max's was Roger's use of *descriptive messages* during the conversation. As their name implies, such messages describe a feeling. If a dad is angry, he says "I'm mad" or "I'm annoyed." If he's disappointed, he uses a statement like the one Roger used toward the end of his conversation with Max: "I think it's important for you to know that I feel hurt that you forgot our date." A *blame message* is an accusation. The speaker acts out his negative emotion by verbally pointing a finger in the child's face and saying, "You let me down" or "You're a bad boy" or "You're acting irresponsibly." And since most dads would rather say nothing than say something as harsh and unforgiving as "You're a bad boy," one drawback of blame messages is that they're great paternal inhibitors.

"Better to bite my tongue and say nothing than sound like a prosecuting attorney," the man concludes, and so the child, who should be—and often for his own good needs to be—admonished is left thinking he got away with something, because Dad can't think of an appropriate way to reprimand him without sounding like a heavy.

Another even more serious drawback of blame messages is that they strike directly at a child's self-esteem. Telling him "You're a bad boy" again and again will make him feel so small and unworthy that eventually he'll conclude, "Dad's right, I am worthless."

And youngsters who think they're worthless usually think that everyone else is. So they don't have any inhibitions about robbing or hurting other people. If you look at the studies of kids who are arrested again and again for vandalism, theft, and assault, you'll see what I mean. The one common denominator, which cuts across differences in race and class and sex, is low self-esteem.

On top of everything else, blame messages don't work. "You're a bad boy" and "You're irresponsible" are statements of opinion and, like all statements of opinion, they leave the door open to argument. Roger can tell Max, "You behaved irresponsibly." But Max could—and, if pressed, probably would—argue for several hours that he didn't. Ricky would've probably taken the same contrary stance the other night if Sam had said, "Rick, I think you're too young to watch *Jaws*."

Descriptive statements work for all the reasons blame statements don't. Because they're descriptions of paternal feeling, for example, they shut the door to argument. While Dad's opinions about irresponsible or inappropriate behavior can be endlessly contested, what can't be argued is the way particular behaviors make Dad feel. There's only one person who can speak on Dad's feelings with authority and that's Dad himself. So when you say to a youngster, "Max, I feel hurt that you forgot our date," you, in effect, give the child nothing to argue about, which puts you in the enviable position of having an uninterrupted run at explaining why you feel the way you do about a particular behavior.

More centrally, descriptive statements also preserve and enhance a child's self-respect because saying "I'm mad" or "I'm upset" implicitly tells a boy or girl, "I feel the way I do because *you matter to me.*" And having been reassured of Dad's concern, a child can hear what comes next without feeling hurt or humiliated, belittled or accused.

An important adjunct to descriptive statements are *I-messages,* such as "I worry that . . ." or "I'm afraid when you . . ." or "I get upset at . . ." And if you stop and analyze a statement like "I'm mad at you because *I'm afraid* that you're doing something that will hurt you," you can see why. The inclusion of the I-message "I'm afraid" not only makes Dad's concern explicit, it also makes an important distinction. It tells the boy or girl, "What Dad's angry at isn't you, but your behavior, because he's afraid it may harm you."

The combination of a descriptive statement and an I-message would have been a big help in resolving Sam's *Jaws* dilemma. He needed to tell Ricky something that wouldn't sound accusatory or threatening to his six-year-old sense of machismo. And a statement like "Rick, *I'm upset* by your anxiety. *I'm worried* that *Jaws* is going to give you nightmares" would have fit the bill on both counts.

The "I'm upset" in the first part of the statement would have described his reaction and established his concern, while the "I'm afraid" in the second part would have made that concern explicit, but in a way that would have entirely sidestepped the issue of Ricky's machismo. He'd have been telling Rick that he wanted to take the video out because he was upset about its effect on him, not because he didn't think Ricky was a big enough boy to watch it.

The combination of a descriptive statement and an I-message would have helped Dave Pullio as well.

The easiest kinds of errors to admit are the ones that arise from caring and concern. And that would have been the very explicit message of a statement like "Keri, I realize I made a mistake: I'm sorry. The reason I got so *angry* with you is I know that bad things can happen to fifteen-year-old girls who stay out late and *I'm worried* that one night one of those bad things will happen to you."

No dad would mind saying "I'm sorry" for caring that much.

Let's see what you've learned from Sam's and Dave's experiences. Imagine that your son has just told you that he and his friends want to take an overnight trip to New York City. Which of the following three statements tells him no in a way that exemplifies Self-expression's "Describe; don't blame" rule?

1. You're only thirteen. Don't you think that's a little young to be going to New York with a bunch of friends?
2. I'd be worried. I wouldn't want anything bad to happen to you and New York is a risky proposition for a thirteen-year-old on his own.
3. Ask your mother.

Though it may not seem so, reply 1 contains a subtle form of finger pointing. "Don't you think that's a little young?" isn't as harsh or directly indicting as "You're a bad boy," but it is an accusation. It says "I think you're too immature" and it would belittle and humiliate a child as much as "Rick, this video's too scary for a six-year-old; I'm taking it out now" would have belittled Ricky.

Reply 3 also is wrong. Not because it's blaming but because it represents a form—in many cases, a too-common form—of paternal indifference. It says, "Look, I've got enough on my mind; don't bother me with your problems."

That leaves the second reply, and it's correct for two reasons. It describes the dad's reaction to the child's request ("I'd be worried"). And, for good measure, it adds an I-message ("I wouldn't want anything bad to happen to you"), which lets the youngster know his request is being denied not because Dad has doubts about his maturity but because Dad's concerned about his safety.

Always acknowledge the child's point of view is Self-expression's second step, and it's important because it tells a chastised or scolded child, "I understand that you have a mind and heart of your own, even though we sometimes disagree with the thoughts and feelings they produce." Three examples of the technique are: "I know you're angry at being grounded but . . ."; "I know you wish you could go tomorrow but . . ."; and "I know you see things differently than I do, but . . ." Each of these statements makes it clear that while Dad disagrees, he disagrees in a way that salutes his boy's or girl's intelligence and independence.

The point-of-view remarks Roger Levine used in his conversation with Max, "I understand being with your friends is important to you," illustrates another important benefit of such remarks. They allow you to avoid the trap of New Father guilt.

"My kids can think anything about me as long as they don't think I sound like a dictator" is a very common paternal sentiment these days. And while, in many ways, it's a noble one, too often it produces the kind of paternal silences that leave a youngster without the guidance and discipline he needs—especially when he does something harmful or injurious. Max's remark at the end of his conversation is an example of how point-of-view statements can make fear of sounding dictatorial or authoritarian groundless. Roger certainly didn't hide his unhappiness at being stood up, but because he took the time to acknowledge Max's feelings about his friends and the party, Max didn't feel a nasty paternal finger was being stuck in his face. Hence, his parting "Thank you."

Sam Aberjanassi's *Jaws* dilemma would also have been easier to resolve if a point-of-view remark had been used.

Obviously, Ricky likes scary movies, and if Sam had acknowledged that preference by saying, "I know you think scary movies are fun, Rick," it would have made him even less likely to resist, particularly if Sam had added, "But *Jaws* is an exceptionally scary movie and I'm worried that watching it will upset you."

A point-of-view remark also would have helped Dave Pullio. Every fifteen-year-old thinks of herself as an apprentice adult, and if Dave had paid his respects to that notion by saying, "Pumpkin, I know you're a big girl now, but . . ." Keri would have been so obviously pleased by his compliment that he wouldn't have had any difficulty putting aside his pride and saying, "I'm sorry, Keri. I made a mistake."

Why don't you try your hand at point-of-view statements now? Imagine that you catch your fourteen-year-old with a cigarette and he says, "So what if I smoke. What do you care? It's my business." Which of these replies acknowledges his perspective but also states your legitimate concern?

1. I don't want you smoking and that's it.
2. I think smoking's bad and I'm worried that it might make you sick.
3. I know you're big enough to make decisions for yourself. But I'm afraid smoking will harm you.

One is obviously wrong. But what about 2? "I'm worried that it might . . ." is an I-message. It objects to smoking on the grounds of personal concern. The dad is saying, "I love you too much to see you hurt yourself like this." But you're right; it doesn't contain a point-of-view remark. Solicitous as it is about the child's well-being, it ignores his thinking about smoking. Three is the only one of the replies that takes that important factor into account. "I know you're big enough . . ." salutes the child's attitude about smoking, while "I'm afraid smoking will . . ." puts Dad's objection to it in the form of an I-message.

One more time. Imagine your youngster has just said, "Dad, can I have an advance on next week's allowance?" Which of the following statements acknowledges the child's point of view while keeping next week's allowance in your pocket until next week?

1. I get upset when you ask for these advances. Your allowance is supposed to last a week, not three days.
2. Your spending habits worry me. If you don't learn to manage money better, I'm afraid you'll find yourself in trouble one day.

3. I know you think your allowance isn't big enough, but the reason I put you on one is that I think it's a good way for you to learn how to budget money.

Though it contains a descriptive message ("I get upset"), 1 is obviously wrong. Two makes you hesitate, however. "I'm afraid that" is a very good example of an I-message, but you're right; it doesn't follow through with a point-of-view remark. Only 3 has that ("I know you think your allowance isn't big enough") as well as a sympathetic I-message ("the reason that I put you on one . . .").

While acknowledging a youngster's point of view lets him know you respect his thinking, paternal criticisms, directives, and discipline are even more acceptable to him when he knows you still recognize and appreciate his good qualities. And that is the point of Self-expression's third rule: *Always balance negative remarks and criticism with a positive statement.* Telling the seven-year-old who's just hit his little brother, "I'm surprised at you; you're usually the family peacemaker," or the ten-year-old who's lost your change on the way home from the store, "That's strange; you're usually so conscientious," is a way of saying, "Despite our current problem, Dad still thinks you have some terrific qualities."

Another reason for Max Levine's unexpected thank you is that, as annoyed as his dad was, he took the time to pay Max a compliment. Roger's "I know you care about Rabbi Goldstein"—and didn't want to disappoint him—let Max know that, even in a moment of anger, his dad hadn't lost sight of Max's thoughtfulness.

Positive statements also help you because they allow you to criticize and reprimand without sounding like a faultfinder, which is another great paternal silencer because faultfinding is not a trait most men admire.

An important corollary to Self-expression's third rule is *be specific* when you're being negative. Make it clear to the boy or girl that your criticism and reprimands are related to a specific situation, incident, or behavior. Otherwise, the child will not think, "I disappointed Dad because I stood him up" (or "flunked math" or "lost his change"); he will think, "I'm a disappointment to Dad, period." In other words, he'll come away thinking that he's just received an open-ended condemnation.

"Ricky, I think you're smart enough to know that *Jaws* is going to give you nightmares. So why don't we turn it off?" is an example of how Sam could have applied the positive rule to his *Jaws* dilemma. An example of how he could have applied all three of Self-expression's rules to that dilemma is a statement like "Rick, I know that you like scary movies. But I think *Jaws* is the exception. It's too scary and I'm worried that if you keep watching it, you're going to get nightmares. What's more, I think you're smart enough to know your old dad's right. So why don't we turn *Jaws* off and find something else to do?"

Sam's opening remark, "I know that . . ." acknowledges Ricky's point of view. "I think *Jaws* is the exception. It's too scary" describes the way he feels about his son's watching the movie. "I'm worried that . . ." puts his paternal concerns into the personal form of an I-message. And "I think you're smart enough . . ." tells Rick even in a difficult situation his dad has one eye firmly fixed on his good qualities.

For Dave Pullio, a statement that incorporates all three of Self-expression's rules would go something like this: "Keri, I'm sorry. I made a mistake. And I know you're a big girl. But I worry when you stay out this late. I'm afraid something bad may happen. And I think you're responsible enough to know my fears aren't groundless."

The first part of Dave's remark—"I'm sorry . . . And I know you're a big girl"—acknowledges Keri's point of view. "I'm sorry" apologizes for a paternal error. "I'm worried" describes a paternal feeling instead of pointing a paternal finger. "I'm afraid" adds an I-message of personal concern. "And I think you're responsible" salutes one of Keri's good qualities. Her dad thinks she's a mature young lady.

One reason Dave and Sam and not Rose Pullio and Olympia Aberjanassi found themselves in these predicaments is that moms tend to exercise foresight. Most of the paternal problem emotions we've been talking about could be avoided if a father exercised a little foresight and avoided the situation that provoked them. Most men tend to leap before they look, but often before stepping into a situation a woman will ask herself, "How will my child react to this?" and "How will his reaction affect me?" Sometimes these questions will lead a mother to conclude that the best way to deal with a situation is to avoid it entirely. I strongly suspect, for example, that this is the strategy Olympia Aberjanassi would have adopted if Ricky had asked her to get *Jaws*. She would have thought about the boy on the beach blanket, put it together with what she knows about her son, and concluded that it would be easier to deal with Ricky's disappointment now than to deal with all the fears and anxieties that would arise later if he got his way.

A classic example of this avoid strategy is the way women often reconnoiter routes to their kids' schools and friends' houses beforehand. Knowing how suggestible kids are, a woman will look for a route that contains a minimum of candy stores and ice-cream parlors, because she knows such a route will cut down on the number of times she'll be asked, "Mom, can I have . . ." when she's taking her child to school or to a playmate's house.

Maternal foresight will also prompt a woman to restructure difficult situations that can't be avoided. An example is the way a friend of my wife's restructured her seven-year-old's visits to the dentist's office after he threw a temper tantrum there.

After analyzing the situation, she decided that two small changes would materially lower the risk of future explosions. One was to announce the visits earlier. Her policy had been to wait until the morning of the visit, because this technique had worked for her eleven-year-old. After the tantrum, however, she decided that maybe a seven-year-old needs more time to prepare himself for the dentist. So she began announcing visits a few days in advance. Her second change was to provide a small treat at the end of each visit. Henceforth, her son was informed, he and Mom would stop off on the way home for a Big Mac or a movie. I can't say her son now loves the dentist above all things, but these changes have made the experience a lot more bearable for him and, of course, for his mother.

A similar display of foresight could have helped Roger Levine avoid that confrontation on his son's front porch. After the first temper tantrum, my wife's friend realized she was putting her seven-year-old in a situation he wasn't old enough to handle. Same-day notice might be fine for an eleven-year-old, but a seven-year-old needed more time to prepare himself for the dentist's chair. Roger made a similar mistake when he assumed an eight-year-old wouldn't need a reminder call about the hockey game.

A week is a long time for a youngster that age. It's easy for him to forget. Had Roger called the night before the hockey game and reminded Max of it, I think he would have found this little extra bit of foresight as effective as the advance notice my wife's friend began giving her seven-year-old.

My advice to Roger has pertinence for every father. A lot of the negative paternal feelings aroused by unmade beds, unwashed dishes, unmowed lawns, and the other "uns" that signal the presence of perennially unfulfilled chores could be avoided if the dad stopped and thought, "Well, maybe my child needs my help to fulfill his responsibilities."

This isn't to say you have to start mowing the lawn for him. But if it's among his Saturday-morning chores and you know that this Saturday his friend Danny is coming over at 10:00 a.m., mention the lawn the night before, and say, "Why don't I wake you up a little early tomorrow, so you'll have the lawn finished by the time Danny arrives?" Similarly, if you know your daughter takes an hour to get ready for a dance and tonight she has one at school, before dinner you might say, "Why don't you get an early start on washing the dishes so you'll have enough time to get yourself ready for tonight?"

Another insight dads could borrow from my wife's friend is to find a way to make difficult situations as pleasant as possible for a child. She did this by adding a treat at the end of the dentist's visit. Roger might have done it by bringing another dad and son along on the pickup. One of Max's objections to going to the hockey game was that he didn't know any of the other kids. Having another child along would have given Max a chance to make a friend on the drive to the game.

Knowing your own tolerance levels and the situations that provoke them also can help avoid negative feelings. Mike Danzig's experience is a case in point. One of the things the Thundertank experience taught Mike is the importance of knowing how to identify a situation that is likely to cause trouble, and the equal importance of taking action quickly. Which is why these days if Davy Danzig appears in the living room, Laser Tag set in hand, Mike will say, "Not in here, Davy. I'm watching the news. If you want to play Laser Tag, please do it in your room."

Of course, some father-child confrontations are unavoidable. And in the next chapter, we're going to look at the skill that will let you deal with them.

C: Balancing Perspectives of Self and Other

The skill of Resolution Negotiation will help fathers find ways out of the inevitable deadlocks and impasses that occur, by learning to fairly balance the father's concerns against the child's.

5

How to Settle Arguments and Fights

On December 5, 1988, Lexington, Massachusetts, gave birth to a second American Revolution. This time, though, the flashpoint wasn't the Village Green, but a pretty white colonial half a mile away on Redcoat Lane, where on that night fourteen-year-old Timothy Cronin looked up from his dinner and said, "Dad, why don't you be a good dad and let me take out the garbage every other day instead of every day?"

Whereupon seventeen-year-old Colleen Cronin looked up from her dinner and said, "Yeah, Dad, why don't you be a doubly good dad and let me wash the dishes every other night instead of every night?"

Whereupon Maureen Cronin looked up from her dinner and said, "Dear, the children want to talk to you about their chores. Don't you have anything to say?"

Whereupon Paul Cronin looked up from his dinner and said, "Yes. Off with their heads."

Within minutes, news of the revolt spread next door to the Santuccis, who were alerted by a very loud bang, which Mary Santucci thought was the sonic boom from a passing jet, until her fourteen-year-old, Whitney, looked up from her dinner and said, "No, Mom. That's Tim Cronin slamming his bedroom door again. He must have had another fight with his father."

By nine that evening, the Warrens, who live at the other end of Redcoat Lane and whose fifteen-year-old, Jed, is Tim Cronin's best friend, also knew of the revolt. And by the morning of the sixth, word of it had spread to the McDonalds on the corner of Bedford and Revere streets, and, by midafternoon, to the Friendlys, on Massachusetts Avenue.

Official Lexington's first news of the uprising came the next day when Alice Kramer, who's Selectwoman for District Four, was told about it by Janet Donovan, who was told by Sarah Murphy, who also does Maureen Cronin's hair.

The fall group didn't learn of the revolt, however, until the following Tuesday, when Paul Cronin arrived for the seventh session, looking more flustered and upset than tyrants are supposed to look.

"Why didn't you use Self-expression?" a puzzled Sam Aberjanassi asked.

"I did, Sam. Well, I did *later*. At first, I got a little carried away."

Doubt clouded Sam's face. "Doesn't Self-expression work, Paul?"

"Sounding thoughtful is hard when you're shouting through a locked bedroom door, Sam."

"Paul," I said. "Can I ask you a question? Why are you turning your family and what sounds like half of Lexington upside down over the issue of garbage removal?"

Paul glowered. "Ron, the issue isn't garbage removal.

I'm not that narrow-minded. The issue is Timothy. I know sometimes I sound harsh when I talk about him, but I have a boy who has all this wonderful potential, and I see him throwing it away and trying to get by on his good looks and charm. My father did the same thing. Jack Cronin could charm the birds off the trees, and the girls . . . well, my dad was a very handsome man. But in his entire life, I never knew him to pay a bill on time. I realize those memories may have created some problem emotions for me. I think they have. But we're not talking about me now; we're talking about my son, whom, in my own imperfect way, I love and whom I see beginning to head down the same road my father took. If I let Tim sweet-talk me out of this chore, like he's sweet-talked me out of every other chore and responsibility I've ever given him, he'll be even more convinced than he already is that the ticket to success in life is a twinkle in the eye and an Ipana smile. This time, once and for all, I'm going to teach him they're not."

"What about your daughter, Colleen?" I said. "Is she just caught in the middle?"

"Her only concern in this argument is fairness, Ron. She wants to make sure she gets whatever deal Tim gets."

I told Paul it sounded as if he and Tim had one of those intractable problems that occasionally arise in every family. "You feel an important moral issue is at stake in the garbage dispute, and it sounds like Tim has dug in his heels, too."

Paul said he had. "He only communicates with me now through his mother and sister."

"Do you know why he's making such a big deal out of his chore schedule?" I asked.

"Taking out the garbage means Tim doesn't leave the house until eight-thirty, which means he misses walking to school with Jed Warren and Billy Cohen. They're his two best friends. You think I ought to bend a little, Ron?"

Ultimately, the only person who can and should answer a question like Paul's is the father who asks it. But in this chapter, we're going to look at a skill that will help you resolve conflicts like the Cronins', where both parties dig in their heels and declare no prisoners will be taken. It's called Resolution Negotiation, and it's the Fatherhood Project's fifth and final skill.

I know negotiation is a word that makes a lot of dads jump, and, in one way or another, it usually does so for the same reason. Because it implicitly grants a measure of equality to a child in disputes, many fathers feel negotiation topples the key domino of paternal authority. And once it's down and off the board, they're afraid the child will push for concession after concession after concession. Give in on garbage today, they think, and six months from now it will be the curfew, a year from now the car, in eighteen months the right to keep a six-pack of beer in the refrigerator—and in two years, all of Southeast Asia up to the Philippines.

The problem with this view—as with so many others about youngsters—is that it overlooks the child's thinking. The rules on garbage, curfew, and car privileges a dad sees as so many fragile dominoes in danger of being toppled are, to a child, tangible proof of Dad's caring. They place him in the center of a known, orderly moral universe constructed out of Dad's love and concern. And, as a general rule, children are not interested in bringing down or rolling up structures that put them under an umbrella of paternal love and concern. Which is why, when a child goes into opposition, it's almost never about Dad's right to create a universe of rules and regulations, but simply about how much room he can have to maneuver within that universe.

Tim Cronin's behavior is an example. He didn't throw down the gauntlet to his father by saying, "No more chores, Dad," or even, "No more garbage, Dad." He only asked for some sort of accommodation on his current schedule. That's not the behavior of a boy who's taken to the barricades with a red flag, but of one who, while mindful and respectful of his father's authority, also has a problem he'd like some help in solving. And if Paul bends a little and gives in to him by negotiating an agreement that gives Tim some of what he wants, Paul will still be able to make his point about responsibility, and, in the process, teach Tim some other, equally important lessons.

One is about fairness. The negotiation process is premised on the belief that the only workable solutions to father-child problems are those that are fair to both disputants. So the child who sees Dad sifting through possible solutions to find one that gives each of them some of what he wants not only begins feeling good about Dad; he begins to learn how important it is to treat people fairly—even people you disagree with. And that's a lesson the youngster will still be benefiting from fifty years later.

Listening carefully, considering the other person's point of view, and all the other skills you've learned in this book are an important part of negotiation. So another thing the technique will let you do is teach your child how to use these skills herself. Watching you use them to understand her point of view will show her how to use them to make the people she talks to feel understood. And the child who knows how to do that not only won't have many problems with her peers and teachers now; she won't have many problems with her spouse or her superiors thirty years from now.

Self-esteem isn't a lesson you teach; it's a quality you nurture. But it deserves to be mentioned in any list of negotiation's attributes because showing a child you're willing to sit down and consider his or her views reveals how seriously you take those views—and, by extension, how seriously you take the child. And this message has just as happy an effect on a boy's or girl's self-esteem as descriptive statements and I-messages.

Kids today see the President of the United States negotiating with the Russians, business negotiating with labor, and ballplayers negotiating with management. So negotiation has the additional advantage of conforming to your child's ideas of how modern authority figures are supposed to behave. Kids expect such figures to exercise guidance and direction, but these days, they expect them to exercise these skills within the context of a warm, friendly give-and-take, and this is the context you create when you settle disputes by:

- picking the right time for a discussion;
- identifying the problem clearly;
- defining the issue;
- discussing it from each disputant's point of view;
- drawing up a list of solutions that reflect those points of view and picking the best one;
- including a review mechanism.

These are Resolution Negotiation's six steps, and to illustrate how the skill works in this chapter, I am—with the fall group's help—going to use it to solve two real problems. One is Paul Cronin's dispute with his son, Tim. The other is John Uterhof's conflict with his daughter, Margery.

Margery, who recently got her driver's license, wants the family Volvo to herself two nights a week. John doesn't have any problem with the time, but he does have a problem with his daughter's wish to have unsupervised use of the car. John says his primary objection to this request is safety. "Bad things can happen to little girls who drive big Volvos," he told me when I asked him why Margery's request was a problem for him. And I know he does have some real concerns in this area. But part of his objection is also rooted in a phenomenon that undermines many father-child negotiations—an unidentified paternal emotion.

In John's case, that emotion is fear. His daughter is sixteen now, which means she's only a few years away from the day she'll be leaving home for good. And one of the things that can make that day seem terrifyingly near to a dad is watching his daughter hop in a car and drive out of his life for a few hours. Yesterday she was his baby, all cuddly and pliant. Today she's already driving with her friends, which means tomorrow she'll be grown up and gone for good.

Of course, John knows he's powerless to stop this process, but like a lot of dads who've been in his position, subconsciously he thinks, "Why not try, anyway? I'll stall on the Volvo." So, also like a lot of dads who've been in his position, John began wondering, "How can I stall?" And the more he wondered, the bigger his Volvo got. One day, it looked like a Mack truck to him, then a Boeing 747, until finally, the night of the negotiation session, he walked out and saw an aircraft carrier in his driveway.

Every father hates to see his kids grow up and away from him. But before our negotiation began, I told John that the danger of a fear like his is that it involves a thing you can't negotiate. There are a number of concrete and tangible concessions a child can make to soothe Dad's concerns about safety, but nothing she can do to assuage his fear about her growing up and leaving him. And when that unidentified fear—or similar unidentified feelings—gets mixed up in the negotiation process, it almost always ends up subverting it.

An issue like car privileges has to be considered on its own merits. Is the child a competent driver? Can she be trusted to be careful with the family car? Will her access to it inconvenience other family members? The dad who sets aside his own feelings and looks at his youngster's request in terms of these concerns will be able not only to use negotiation to settle the dispute but also to solve a problem that often worries men with teenage children: How can I give my youngster the freedom she wants and needs and still be able to exercise the control she needs?

Dads with fifteen-year-olds know that in order to learn and grow, their kids need freedom to make their own decisions. But they also know that even very intelligent, conscientious fifteen- and sixteen-year-olds can, out of a combination of inexperience and immaturity, sometimes make very bad, even harmful, decisions for themselves.

Negotiation can help a man resolve this control-versus-freedom dilemma. Making a youngster's rights a subject of bargaining will show her that you feel she's old enough now to have a voice in deciding how late she stays out, which elective she takes next fall, or whether she gets the Volvo. But negotiation also ensures that whatever decisions are made are made under Dad's mature and experienced eye.

Now, let's look at the six steps of Resolution Negotiation. Step One, *Pick the right time,* reflects the commonsensical notion that the best time to talk to a child about anything is when he's relaxed. And one way to determine that is by looking at what's happening in his life. If the youngster had a grueling forty-five-minute history test this afternoon, or if he's facing one tomorrow, wait and bring up your problem another time. I'd also give this advice to the dad whose child has college boards at the end of the week or who is angry about a fight with a girlfriend. The youngster who has a date or a dance in an hour or two isn't going to be in a mood to talk about a mutual problem tonight, either.

The same is true for the ten-year-old who's sitting knotted up in a ball on the couch, or who's drumming her fingers nervously on the kitchen table, or whose fists are knotted, jaw is clenched, or breathing is shallow. These are all signs of an inner anxiety and turmoil, and while they may not have anything to do with you or your mutual problem, they're going to affect the child's ability to discuss it openly and freely. The boy or girl who glances around when you bring up a problem or who keeps trying to change the subject or who turns on the TV or who keeps looking at a book or magazine also is saying, "Not tonight, Dad."

Conversely, the tilt of a head or body toward you is a signal of a child who is saying, "Yes, Dad, I would like to talk tonight." The youngster who suddenly looks alert or who begins asking questions, who gets up and shuts off the TV or puts down her book or magazine is saying the same thing.

These are all small points, but they can have a big influence on your ability to negotiate, so it's worthwhile keeping them in mind.

Step Two, *Identify the problem,* brings us to the heart

of the negotiating process: getting a handle on the issue in dispute. In some instances, this will be easy because the problem walks up and announces itself. The child who says,"Dad, I want a later curfew" or "Dad, I want to cross the street by myself," is saying very clearly, "Dad, I have a problem I want to discuss with you." The father who walks into his seventeen-year-old's room and immediately thinks, "Enough is enough," also knows immediately he has a problem. Paul's and John's problems are both examples of this kind of easy-to-identify, high-profile issue, and they account for between 60 and 70 percent of father-child disputes.

In the other 30 to 40 percent, the man's unawareness of his hidden agenda or his child's makes the problem harder to pinpoint. If you don't know what you're feeling, you won't think to ask yourself, "Why am I feeling this way?," which means you may never get to the issue that's bothering you. So the appropriate question for the dad who notices himself developing a sudden vulnerability to the Rubber Band Syndrome or spending an increasing amount of his time thinking about lawn furniture or his garage would be "Am I being bothered by an upset I haven't identified?" And the appropriate way to answer it is Self-awareness, in the form of a response notebook where you can track your reactions for a week or two.

This is what Allen Gillis, one of the dads in the spring group, did when he noticed himself jumping on his two teenagers for anything and everything. And within days a pattern began to emerge. Allen's entries showed that his overreactions increased markedly in the evening when he saw his wife, who worked all day too, standing at the kitchen sink washing the dishes while his kids sat talking at the table, and on Saturday mornings, when he brought the wash down to the laundry room while they lay sleeping in their beds. And after thinking about this pattern for a while Allen decided his overreactions were an expression of a feeling and a problem he didn't know he'd had: he was furious at his kids for not helping more around the house.

Self-awareness, though, in a different form, would also be the appropriate tool for the father who finds himself unable to make the smallest concessions on issues like curfews, TV privileges, clothing, study hours, or bedtimes. This kind of paternal intransigence is usually a signal of a hidden agenda, which is linked to some secret paternal fear, anxiety, or resentment. And the best way to find out what it is, is to sit down and ask yourself, "Is there anything in my past, my values, or my nightmares which makes this a difficult issue for me to think about objectively?"

Joe Davis, one of the fathers in last fall's group, did this when the request of his seventeen-year-old, Jonathan, for an increase in his car privileges from one to two nights a week made him dig in his heels. After some serious introspection, Joe realized that his intransigence grew out of his own childhood experiences. His family couldn't afford a car when he was growing up, and he resented it that Jonathan seemed to think twice-weekly car privileges were part of his natural birthright.

The youngster who makes unreasonable requests or who keeps breaking agreements or who is always demanding new concessions usually also has a hidden agenda, and the appropriate tool for handling it is understanding Hidden Messages. A case in point is the way Jim Mansuto, another former program dad, used the skill to handle his daughter Tracy's request for a phone of her own. Since Tracy was only eight, this demand struck Jim as outrageous, but he also knew that outrageous demands often are a way-station on the road to hidden agendas. So one day while they were discussing the appropriateness of an eight-year-old's having her own phone, Jim began reflecting Tracy's feelings, and within a few minutes, the real issue emerged. What Tracy was saying with her demand wasn't "Dad, I want a new phone" but "Dad, I think you buy my sister, Denise, more clothes than you buy for me."

Step Three in Resolution Negotiation is *Define the issue* that's been identified clearly and concretely. And first and foremost this means separating out those aspects of a problem which *can't* be negotiated, like fear of losing your daughter, and reducing it to something tangible that can, like, should Margery Uterhof be given car privileges two nights a week? If the child presents you with a problem that's half concrete and half fears and anxieties or jealousies, do the same for him or her. For example, if an eight-year-old says, "Dad, I want to be able to do everything Sharon does," tell her, "Honey, I can't wave a wand over your head and turn you into a twelve-year-old. But maybe I can expand some of your rights and privileges. So why don't you tell me what you want and we'll talk about it?"

Next, state the defined problem in simple, concrete terms, so everyone understands what it is. If the issue is yours, saying "So now you understand why attitude X or behavior Y is a problem for me" will leave the child in no doubt about the source of your upset. If the problem is his, saying "So you feel entitled to privileges A, B, and C" will let him know that he's been heard and understood. Sometimes defining a problem leads directly to negotiating about it. Other times, it doesn't; if the child says he doesn't want to talk about it any more tonight, or if you sense he doesn't, don't push, but do make a discussion date before the conversation ends.

A child who hears a problem defined but doesn't hear Dad say, "Let's talk about it Wednesday night," is going to simmer and stew until he gets a bee in his bonnet; and children with bees in their bonnets are a leading cause of premature aging and ulcers in adult males.

Wally Malloy, another former program dad, is a case in point. Wally got a bee in *his* bonnet about his twelve-year-old daughter Ali's preference for mismatched purple and white socks. Don't ask me why he did, he just did. Wally was like that. One Monday morning his bee's buzz grew so loud that Wally imposed a ban on such attire, which then put a bee—a very big bee—in Ali's bonnet. And since Wally imposed the ban without announcing that in a week or so he planned to negotiate a sartorial agreement everyone could live with, Ali's bee got madder and madder as the days passed, until finally it flew up and stung poor Wally. Out of spite, Ali went out and got an earring put in her nose.

Step Four is *Discuss the problem from each disputant's perspective.* And to illustrate how it works, let's step inside the session on negotiation and watch while John Uterhof and Paul Cronin define their respective problems and the issues those problems raise for them and for their kids.

John, who spoke first on this particular night, defined the principal issue between himself and Margery as whether she should or shouldn't have access to the family car two nights a week.

"From my perspective," he said, "the most important issue is safety. The Volvo really is big, and I honestly do worry about how well equipped a sixteen-year-old with two months of driving experience is to drive it. Time might also be a problem. I don't have any difficulties with the two nights, but if one of them fell on a weekend night, it would be inconvenient for Joan and me. I also have some worries about Margery's behavior. She's not irresponsible, thank God, but sixteen-year-olds do have a habit of spilling things like Cokes and popcorn and ketchup from hamburgers onto car seats. And I'm very fond of my Volvo. I want to keep it looking neat and clean.

"For Margery," John added, "the paramount concern is freedom. As a sixteen-year-old with a license, she feels entitled to have the car to herself a few nights a week. I think, no. I'm sure another issue for her would be peer relations. Her two best friends each get their family cars one or two nights a week, and Margery feels she'd lose face with them if she didn't. I imagine a third concern for her would be simple convenience. Instead of having to depend on me or her mother for a ride, if she wanted to visit a friend or go to the mall, she could just get in the car and go."

Next, I asked Paul Cronin to define the Cronin family's sanitation problem from his and then Tim's perspective.

Paul frowned. "I've already told you, Ron. The main point for me is to teach Tim a lesson about responsibility. And I came in here feeling like a hero for sticking to my guns and trying to do that, despite all the flak I've gotten. Now, it suddenly sounds as if I'm being accused of having a . . . what did you call it? A hidden agenda."

"Paul, I'm not accusing you. And you should feel proud. By sticking to your guns, you are doing something important for Tim. I just don't want you to confuse a legitimate paternal right and even duty—to teach responsibility—with a paternal fear that will end up making you trip all over yourself and alienate Tim in the process. Okay?"

"Okay."

"Now what other concerns do you have?"

"Well, there's the practical one of getting the garbage out of the house. Five people produce a great deal of trash in a twenty-four-hour period. I'm not sure what name I'd put on my other concern, but it boils down to the fact that Maureen and I both work and our kids should be willing to help us. We're a family, and families pull together.

"From Tim's perspective, as I've already said, the main issue is Jed and Billy and the walk to school. I suppose peer relations or, probably more accurately, peer one-upsmanship could also be called a concern. Neither Jed nor Billy has garbage chores, and I know that it miffs Timothy to think he has to do something his friends don't. Peer relations would be a second issue for Timothy. The third is his vanity, which he gets from his mother."

"Paul, what has vanity got to do with garbage?"

"Once in a while the shopping bags we use as trash liners have leaked and stained Tim's pants—not badly, but he's gotten very upset about it.

"For Colleen, the principal issue is fairness. She doesn't want her little brother getting any breaks that she doesn't also get. And I don't blame her. I'm the same way."

Step Five in Resolution Negotiation is *Draw up a list of solutions that reflect the thinking of the disputants and pick one.* And since everyone in the group now knew the thinking of the parties in the Cronin and Uterhof disputes, I opened this step up to everyone. We began with the Uterhofs' problem.

"I'm with Margery on the two nights," Roger Levine said. "She's sixteen, why not? Also, I can understand why

John's nervous about safety. So I'd limit Margery's driving privileges to early evenings twice a week. Also, one other alternative would be to give her one weekend afternoon. Either arrangement would meet most of Margery's requirements. Also, it would give John a little peace of mind."

Sam Aberjanassi, who spoke next, said in the interests of safety he'd impose one more restriction on Margery. For the next six months, until she got a little more driving experience, he wouldn't allow her to take the car beyond Canton (the Uterhofs' hometown) without her father's permission. "I'd also put Boston proper entirely off limits to her," Sam added.

Dave Pullio came up with a novel solution to John's neatness concerns. "I'd make Margery wear a giant bib when she eats in the car," he said.

Dave was only joking, of course. But his joke makes an important point about negotiation. Humor in the form of wacky suggestions is a good way to keep the negotiation atmosphere light, loose, and creative.

I had a more serious proposal for John. I suggested keeping a supply of paper towels in the car trunk and making it a rule that everyone have a towel on their lap before opening Big Macs and Double Whoppers. Combined with Sam's and Roger's suggestions, it seemed to me my idea would give both Uterhofs a satisfying agreement. John concurred when I pointed this out to him.

"It would give Margery the access to the car she wanted," he said, "but the restrictions on its use and how food is to be eaten in it would satisfy my concerns."

Paul Cronin's problem, which came up for discussion next, proved a little more difficult to solve. When Sam Aberjanassi suggested that one possible solution to it would be making garbage removal a joint father-son chore, Paul snapped, "That's ridiculous, Sam. Taking the garbage out twice a week means I'll have to get up a half hour early twice a week, and my days are all pretty long as it is.

"Besides, if I let Tim have two days off, I'll also have to let Colleen. You can't ask me to come home to a sink full of dishes two nights a week. And I can't ask my wife, Maureen, to wash them. She works all day, too."

"Wait a minute." It was John Uterhof. "Paul, I remember your saying that Maureen's mother lives with you. Can't she do the dishes two nights a week?"

Paul sighed. "John has a good memory."

Paul wasn't happy about my suggestion—replacing the shopping bags with trash liners—either. But when I asked him to measure the few extra cents they'd cost against the ill feeling the garbage dispute was producing, he relented and agreed.

I should point out that in real life, problems rarely are solved as swiftly as John's and Paul's. Without a group of able assistants, a father and child have to draw up a list of four or five solutions which represent their respective viewpoints, then go through them and select the one that best meets both their needs or combine two or three into a mutually agreeable solution.

Two other points to keep in mind about negotiating are:

Stay cool. The adult sets the tone in bargaining sessions. And if he begins getting annoyed—as Paul did at Sam—it will either annoy or intimidate his partner. Either way, the negotiation will fail.

Be realistic. Negotiations rarely produce perfect solutions. So when a father or a child makes perfection the only acceptable goal, the perfect becomes the enemy of the good. The essence of a good negotiation is that it lets everyone win a little. And that's what both John's and Paul's agreements do.

Though a dad should never sell a particular solution to a child, sometimes youngsters become so intent on getting 100 percent of what they want, that they don't see all the concessions they've been granted. And here's where your Self-expression skill can help you in negotiations. A statement like "I understand your position and I know that this agreement doesn't entirely satisfy it, but I'm willing to make some sacrifices to give you a big part of what you want" will remind the youngster how far you've bent to give him some of the things he wants.

Occasionally, a dad should also remind himself of what he's gained from his agreement, because when both disputants feel they've won something big in a settlement, they develop a vested interest in upholding its provisions.

The flip side of this axiom is that when one of the parties feels unfairly treated, unhappiness eventually unravels the agreement. There are a number of reasons why injustices occur, but in one way or another, almost all of them are rooted in inexperience. Father and child sit down with every intention of shaping a mutually acceptable agreement, but being new to the negotiation process, they let subtle biases slip in that tilt the accord in one or the other party's favor.

A case in point is the father and daughter who settle their conflict about the daughter's play clothes through an exchange of promises. The child promises to be extra careful playing if Dad promises not to complain every time he sees her in the backyard with a new coat or pair of shoes. On the face of it this sounds like a fair agreement, which is why the dad proposed it. But, in fact, it's subtly biased against him; he's given in to his child's desire to play in her new clothes. And the first time she comes in with mud on her new shoes or coat—as sooner or later she will—Dad's going to realize this and get very angry. And sooner or later that anger is going to destroy their accord.

Now let's see what this father's experience has taught you about identifying biased agreements. Imagine that your daughter decides to lose ten pounds she doesn't need to lose by skipping breakfast. And you're so alarmed by her decision, you propose a negotiation, the end result of which is she agrees to resume eating her Wheaties, in return for a $7.50 increase in her weekly allowance. Is this agreement biased or unbiased?

Correct, it's biased toward her. In effect, you're bribing her to eat. And bribery isn't a parenting policy that serves father or children very well.

One more: Suppose your son has a problem getting up in the morning and, since it's begun making him late for school, you suggest a negotiation that produces the following result: you bring a glass of orange juice to his bedside each morning in return for which he answers your first wake-up call.

At first glance, this agreement may look biased. It turns you into a butler. But since your child's also making a sacrifice—he agrees to get up the first time you ask—it actually lets both of you win a little and that is the hallmark of an unbiased agreement.

Finally, imagine that your son asks to go to a rock concert that will keep him out an hour after his curfew time. However, when he reminds you how diligent he's been about his chores, and how that reflects on his general trustworthiness, you relent and give him permission to go. A biased or unbiased agreement?

Correct, it's unbiased because it lets everyone win a little. Your son wins because he gets to go to his concert and you win because you get some peace of mind, having been reminded of how lucky you are to have such a responsible child.

One last point about Step Five: whatever agreement a father and child make should be put in writing. This may sound officious, but if differences in interpretation arise—especially over what constitutes an infraction of the rules—the two of you will have something tangible to consult. Another way to avoid future arguments about what you meant when you said "A" and what your child meant when he said "B" is to spell out the agreement's provisions very specifically.

In John's case this would mean including in his accord with Margery which weeknight and weekend day she gets the car, the amount of time she gets it for, and the limitations he's imposed on its use; in Paul's case, which two days a week he'll be getting up a half hour early and which two nights his mother-in-law will take over from Colleen at the sink.

The other thing that needs to go into the agreement in writing is a *review date.* Father and child should specify that on a certain date three or four weeks hence they will sit down and examine how well their accord is working. This is Step Six in Resolution Negotiation, and it's an important one because none of us has perfect future sight, and a review mechanism provides a way of dealing with the unforeseen consequences that flow from almost every accord. What if Paul discovers, for example, that the two days he's agreed to take out the garbage have become inconvenient because his firm now wants him in the office those two days instead of out on the road selling? Or

Margery discovers that Canton is even smaller than she thought and after two weeks of driving around it, she's becoming claustrophobic. Knowing that a date has been set aside to deal with such problems will make Paul and Margery much more likely to sit on their unhappiness until the review, instead of throwing up their hands and saying, "I'm breaking this agreement. It just doesn't work for me." Which, happily enough, brings me to the question of infringements generally.

Dads being dads, infringements usually aren't a problem for them. But kids being kids, there will be times when commitments to pick up rooms and wash dishes and be home at a certain hour are forgotten. How you deal with such memory lapses depends on their frequency. Initially, I'd recommend a policy of gentle but firm reminders: if the towel doesn't go back on the rack as promised, say, "Hey, remember our agreement; you get the bathroom to yourself for fifteen minutes every morning in return for putting the towels back." If the forgetfulness persists, escalate a step to self-reminders. Tell the child you hate to nag over a little thing like a bathroom towel, so maybe it would be a good idea if he posted a note in the bathroom which says, "I promised Dad I'd always put the towels on the rack."

If the forgetfulness threatens to become chronic, escalate to Step Three: a full-dress sit-down talk, during which you remind the amnesiac of his promise to put the towels on the rack in return for your promise to give him fifteen undisturbed minutes each morning to comb his hair.

If, despite the best efforts of medical science, chronic amnesia develops, some kind of consequence has to be devised. The best time to deal with this problem is beforehand, when you're drawing up the agreement. Mention to your partner that since contractual infringements have been known to occur, it might be a good idea for him to decide now what would be a fair consequence if he breaks the agreement and then write his suggestion into the contract.

I know a lot of dads feel asking a child such a question is asking for trouble, because he'll try to get himself off lightly. But I think this attitude is unfair to kids. Boys and girls have a strong sense of justice; it's why kids are always saying, "It's not fair," and they are just as willing to apply the dictates of this sense to themselves as to a parent who says, "I don't care if I do usually let you watch that TV program, you can't tonight." So if you open up the issue of agreement infringements to a youngster, you'll find that the consequences he suggests are often just as tough as the ones you suggest.

Besides, giving a boy or girl a voice in such decisions has important practical and developmental benefits. Practically, knowing that he's played a part in making the decision makes a youngster much more willing to accept a consequence uncomplainingly. While, developmentally, asking him, "What do you think is a fair consequence for an infringement?" forces him to think about what he's done, and such thinking is how children learn to reason morally.

Parent-imposed punishments are a bad idea for all the reasons kid-imposed ones are a good idea. They produce resistance. Where does Dad get off acting like a dictator, the boy or girl thinks. And they don't teach a child anything more than a basic Pavlovian association between misbehavior and punishment.

One important note: in a more perfect world, every father-child dispute would be settled by negotiation that gives both parties a fair share of what they want. But in this imperfect world, sometimes a father's moral responsibility to his child will put him in conflict with the fairness doctrine. An obvious example is alcohol. I suppose an argument can be made on the grounds of fairness that a sixteen- or seventeen-year-old has a right to keep a six-pack of beer in the refrigerator. But I think anyone who has seen the statistics on alcohol-related deaths and injuries among teenagers would feel that when an issue poses a threat to a child's life and limb, fairness has to ride in the back of the bus.

In such cases, however, you should try to respond to the youngster's wish in some other way. Say, for instance, he'd like to be able to see his girlfriend on weeknights, but you think it's a bad idea. Inviting the girlfriend over one night for dinner would be a way of showing the youngster that you're trying to be fair within the limits of your responsibility to him as a parent.

Also, don't feel every dispute has to be negotiated. There are lots of times when you can and should just say no. For example, if the rule is bedtime at nine, and the child's ignoring it, just tell her, "Bedtime is at nine, young lady, and it's now nine o'clock." Or "Please, I know you have a lot to do today, but the rule in this house is that everyone picks up his own room." Kids will generally accept your assertions of authority as being fair as long as you give a reason when one is needed, grant them a hearing when they want one, and are willing to try to work out a reasonable solution if a conflict does develop.

Now that you know how the project's skills work, in the next section of the book we're going to show you how to use them to solve the challenges that are part of being a father today.

Part II

The Skills and Child Development

*How the skills can
be used to foster three
dimensions of development
that are especially important
to fathers: Moral Growth,
Academic Achievement,
and Sex-Role Identification*

6

How to Show a Child How to Say No to Alcohol, Drugs, and Sex

Groups come and go, but the men in them never really leave your life, and the first man from the fall group to reenter mine was Dave Pullio, who arrived in my outer office one bitterly cold January afternoon three weeks after graduation, wrapped in an enormous black car coat and looking even more troubled than he had sounded on the phone that morning when he'd called from the Arlington police station to say his son Dominick had been in an accident, but was unhurt.

Since it was 6:00 a.m., I hadn't pressed Dave for details. But the more I thought about our conversation, the more ominous it had seemed. Was anyone with Dominick? Had they been hurt? What were he and Dave doing in the Arlington police station—and at that hour of the morning? I suspected that the answers to these questions wouldn't be happy ones, and as soon as I saw Dave in my outer office that afternoon, I knew I was right.

"Have you been waiting long? I got held up in a class."

"Just a few minutes, Ron. Greta got me some coffee."

"Good. You look tired." As I led Dave into my office, I realized he also looked frightened.

"Sorry to bother you at home, Ron. What happened is that Dominick—you remember Dom, my seventeen-year-old . . ."

"Dave, why don't you sit down and take your coat off."

Dave looked down at his feet and discovered to his surprise that he was still standing. "Oh, yeah. That's the state that kid has me in."

"What happened?"

"What happened is very simple. Last night Dominick was arrested by the Arlington police for drunken driving and reckless endangerment. I've been at the lawyer's office with him all morning. We—he has to be in court Tuesday."

For a minute or so, the only sound in my office came from the ticking of a clock on the wall and the rumbling of a trolley car winding its way up Commonwealth Avenue in the pale light of a winter afternoon.

"I'm sorry," I said finally, "for you and Dom. I know he's a good boy."

"Last night at the police station, I was so furious I thought I was going to kill him."

"I can imagine."

"But now all I feel is exhausted. I can barely talk."

"I understand. Take your time, Dave."

Dave needed nearly a half hour to finish his story. But before he'd gotten a quarter of the way through, I knew I was hearing another variation on that familiar tale of our time, the weak but well-meaning teenager. Dominick Pullio *is* a good boy, but, like so many kids today, he lacks that firm sense of right and wrong that allows a youngster to say *no* when all around him are saying yes, and the independence of mind and heart to stand on his nos when the yeses of others turn to dares and taunts. The night before, Dom and his mother and father had learned what can happen when this kind of inner moral compass is missing.

Dave explained that the evening had begun with an invitation from Nick Plazzo, one of the neighborhood kids, to go drinking. "The stupid thing is that Dominick hates alcohol. Even at weddings I have a tough time getting him to take wine for the toast. But Nick is sort of a big deal in our neighborhood. I don't understand that. He looks like Max Headroom to me. Imagine that, Ron, an Italian kid who looks like Max Headroom. But Dom and his friends all think Nick is the original Mr. Cool."

"So," I said, "faced with the choice of doing something he doesn't like or being thought uncool by Mr. Cool himself, Dom decided to accept Nick's invitation and go drinking."

"I wish that was the worst of it. Nick's next big idea was that he and Dom and the two other kids they were with would pile into *my* car, which Dominick had last night, and visit some girls up in Arlington who Mr. Cool had a line on. Coming home from the police station at six-thirty this morning, Dom told me he was still sober enough at that point to know he shouldn't get behind the wheel of a car. But he was afraid to say no because—"

"Because he was afraid of what Nick and the other boys would say."

"Right. Anyway, the boys and my car didn't get any farther than the Arlington line. At the Rotary on Route Two, they hit another car. It was an Arlington police car."

"Not a good choice, Dave."

"Not a good choice at all."

Dave paused for a moment, then said, "I do see a silver lining in this mess. It'll give me a chance to teach Dominick a lesson about right and wrong he won't forget. This morning I told him he was grounded indefinitely and that he could forget about the senior prom and he could also forget about his graduation ceremony. I'll have Somerville High mail him his diploma. I figure he'll be able to pick it up at the post office sometime around 2001 or 2002."

"You're really furious at him, aren't you?"

"Jesus, Ron, wouldn't you be? He could have killed one of those cops last night. I get sick every time I think about it."

"Yes, I'd be mad at him, very mad."

"He's not a baby anymore. He's seventeen. Imagine that—seventeen and he still doesn't know right from wrong."

"And you think grounding him into the next century will teach him?"

"What do you think?"

Dave looked over at the bookcase, where the present the fall group had given me was sitting.

"How do you like your Red Sox cap, Ron?"

"I've got it out on display."

Dave shook his head and sighed again. "Look, I've got enough doubts about what I said I'm going to do to want to come and talk to you."

"I always said you had good instincts, Dave. You should listen to them more often."

"Suppose you explain what they're telling me now, Dr. Levant."

"All right, Mr. Pullio, I will. I think one thing they're telling you is that what you're proposing won't work. The next time Nick asks Dom to go drinking, the threat of your disapproval may make Dominick think, 'I'd better not. If Dad finds out, he'll have a fit.' But the time after that, he'll think, 'Maybe Dad won't find out,' and the time after that, 'Who cares what Dad thinks.' Which is to say, Dave, your instincts are telling you that in a straight-out contest between peer pressure and your disapproval, your disapproval loses nine out of ten times.

"I think your instincts are also telling you that the only person who will effectively make Dom say no to alcohol or drugs or illicit sex—and keep him saying no—however much Nick or his other friends goad him, is Dom. And if this incident does have a silver lining, it's that you now have a chance to help Dom develop the moral compass he'll need to do that.

"Do you remember when we talked about Self-expression? I said there was a common denominator that linked troubled kids of both sexes and all races, income groups, and ethnic backgrounds."

Dave brightened. "Oh, yeah. You said troubled kids had such lousy opinions of themselves that they didn't care what they did to themselves or to other people. Maybe you could call up Nick Plazzo's father and tell him that for me."

"There's a flip side to this axiom, Dave, and it's that kids who like themselves—in other words, kids with high self-esteem—do care. This quality acts like a moral compass, because the child who's used to feeling good about himself is reluctant to risk that good feeling by doing something that will make him feel bad about himself—whether it is getting drunk or doing drugs or being unkind or unfair to the people around him.

"The corollary to these axioms is that punishments have to be chosen very carefully. Belittling or humiliating a youngster—in other words, punishing his self-esteem as well as his crime—only ends up aggravating his misbehavior because the lower his opinion of himself sinks, the less he cares about what he does to himself or to other people. Conversely, punishments that preserve and enhance self-esteem create the kind of environment where disappointing himself by misbehaving becomes far more important to a youngster than disappointing Nick Plazzo.

"High self-esteem is the key, but it's not the only element in the compass. You and Rose, and Dom's uncles and aunts and teachers, and the people on Wall Street, in Washington and in Hollywood also have an influence on it. You're all Dom's role models and opinion shapers, and if you collectively tell him, say, that independence is bad and conformity is good, Dom's going to have a harder time saying no when everyone else is chipping in to buy a gram of cocaine. And if some of you say drug use is bad, but wink at it by depicting the people who use it as cool and hip, you're going to make it even harder for Dom to say no.

"You're sending your boy into a society that's full of mixed messages, not only about drugs, but about sex, greed, selfishness, egotism, and a lot of other things that were considered commonsense matters of bad and good when we were kids, Dave. And if you want Dom to navigate through it in a way that does him—and you—proud, you need to give him a sturdy sense of right and wrong, and, just as important, the independence of heart and mind to use what he knows. That's why I think the best thing I can do for you today is show you some things that will let you help Dom begin developing his own moral compass. And since self-esteem really is the key ingredient, why don't we start with it?"

Dave suddenly looked very wary.

"Ron, promise me, you're not about to tell me the way to make Dom feel good about himself is for me to go home and tell him, 'All is forgiven. I think you're great.' "

"No, what I'm about to tell you is how to give Dominick the punishment he deserves—and needs, incidentally—but in a way that will preserve and enhance his self-esteem, and therefore preserve and promote the moral qualities that flow from it, like a sense of respect for oneself and others, a sense of responsibility, fairness, and consideration."

I told Dave about *respect-oriented* discipline. It consists of four steps, the first of which, *Accept the feeling but not the behavior*, is a variation on the listening skills and is designed to reflect the fact that an awful lot of problem behaviors arise from legitimate feelings and motivations.

Dominick's incident is a good example. Dominick said yes to Nick because he wanted to be liked by him. And Dom has a perfect right to that desire, just as the eight-year-old whose sister spills milk over his new Batman comic book has a perfect right to be mad at her. What Dominick doesn't have a right to do, though, is get drunk and behave irresponsibly. The same is true for that angry eight-year-old. Mad as he is at his sister, he doesn't have a right to haul off and slug her.

Accepting the feeling but not the behavior means acknowledging the legitimacy of an unruly child's motivations in disciplinary situations, which preserves his self-respect. But it also means criticizing the misbehaviors those motivations produce. So the youngster is left in no doubt that, while his feelings are respected, his behavior isn't.

An example of how this technique works would be telling Dominick, "Dom, I know you want Nick and the other kids to like you, but you shouldn't have allowed that desire to talk you into going drinking with them last night." This tells Dom that Dave understands and approves of his motivations, but he finds his behavior unacceptable and deeply distressing. The dad who says to his angry eight-year-old, "You have a perfect right to be mad at your sister for spilling milk over your comic book, but you can't hit her," sends the same validating, but critical message.

This means that Dom and this eight-year-old will still end up feeling pretty good about themselves, and it also has another effect: the dad who always takes the time in disciplinary situations to distinguish between legitimate feelings and motives and illegitimate behaviors is also setting an example of thoughtfulness and consideration, which is going to have an influence on his youngster's behavior with others.

It's quite possible, for instance, that Colleen Cronin will behave differently with her friends because of the way her father, Paul, handled a shopping spree. Colleen was supposed to spend $300 on her prom outfit and she ended up spending $565.

Paul had told his daughter, "Colleen, I know how much the senior prom means to you. But we agreed on a three-hundred-dollar spending limit and you've gone way over that. I'm very angry."

If you think about this statement for a moment, I think you'll find that it not only distinguishes between Colleen's valid feelings about the prom, and her behavior; it also sets a good example for her.

The next time Colleen's angry or upset with a friend, she's very likely to remember how her dad behaved in a similar situation with her, and she'll follow his example. Which is to say, no matter how angry or annoyed she is, Colleen won't call her friend a "creep" or a "nerd" or a "jerk" or do or say anything else that would disparage or denigrate that friend. She'll state her anger appropriately and forcefully, but her friend will emerge from the confrontation with her self-esteem intact and, I suspect, her admiration for Colleen enhanced.

The same is true for that angry eight-year-old. Mad as he may get at his sister, if she spills milk on Batman one more time, he's likely to remember his dad's example and express his anger in a more considerate way.

Dominick, too, could learn these things from his accident, provided that Dave was willing to change his punishment.

I knew that Dave was thinking, "Dominick got drunk last night and could have killed an Arlington policeman. He deserves to be punished severely," and he is right. But if he wants Dom to emerge from this incident still thinking well of himself and with a little more moral awareness than he has now, he has to be disciplined in a way that he feels is *fair*. This is the second step in respect-oriented discipline, and it's a step Dave was overlooking. Putting a ban on the senior prom and keeping Dom away from his graduation ceremony would seem unfair to him. That, in fact, was what Dom had told his father at the lawyer's office.

"And what did you tell him?" I asked Dave.

" 'You're in no position to bargain with me this morning, pal.' "

"You know, Paul also felt a strong punishment was

in order when Colleen told him she'd gone two hundred and sixty-five dollars over her spending limit."

But Paul also learned a valuable lesson from that last session on negotiation. He knew that if Colleen was going to continue thinking, "Dad respects me and is fair," she'd have to be given a voice in deciding her fate. So when she came down to breakfast the morning after the spree, Paul told her about the negotiating techniques he'd learned in the program and said, "Instead of my disciplining you, why don't we use these techniques to devise a punishment that will satisfy us both." And that's what they did. At breakfast the next day, Colleen suggested the $265 be deducted from her allowance in installments. Paul countered by proposing she take the money out of her savings account and pay him back immediately. And after some bargaining back and forth they agreed on a compromise. Colleen would pay half the money back now, and the other half would be deducted from her allowance in weekly installments.

Colleen still isn't especially happy about having to return the $265. But this incident has taught her that when she steps over the line and misbehaves, her father will treat her fairly. And that realization not only has left her feeling pretty good about herself and Paul, it's also left her feeling pretty good about the principle of fairness. And in time, Paul's going to see that feeling reflected in Colleen's relationships with other people.

A negotiated punishment will leave Dom feeling the same way, particularly if Dave and he followed three rules in shaping his punishment. The first is that the consequence should be appropriate to his crime. One problem with Dave's punishment is that it isn't appropriate. Telling Dominick he can't go to the senior prom because he got drunk and hit a police car is like warning a ten-year-old that if he leaves his bike out and it gets stolen, he can't go to the movies for a month. There's no logical connection between misbehavior and punishment. And if a child can't find a logical link between his wrongdoing and his discipline, not only will he be more likely to resist the discipline, he'll be more likely to feel himself unfairly treated.

You should also make sure the punishment is positive. Paul did this by telling Colleen she could donate $15 of her $265 debt to the Lexington United Way, which gave Colleen a chance to do something that would make her feel good about herself. Contributing money to the Arlington Police Athletic League or volunteering some after-school time to a drug-rehabilitation center or a church group would be a logical consequence of Dom's misbehavior and would give him a chance to feel good about himself with all the happy effects that would have on his self-esteem. Dave should just be sure he also lets Dom have a say in selecting whatever disciplinary action is taken.

Putting a finite limit on whatever punishment emerges from your negotiation is also important. Paul did this by telling Colleen that once her debt was repaid, her punishment would be over, and he knew that added to her sense of being dealt with justly. What Dom did was a lot more serious, but not only will an open-ended grounding add to his feeling that Dad's unfair; it will also boomerang on Dave because it will change the focus of the dispute.

As time passes, the issue will be less and less Dominick's behavior, and more and more Dave's treatment of it. Dom will complain about Dave's unfairness to his mother, Rose, to Keri, to his uncle Joe, and to everyone else who will listen, and they'll all turn around and tell Dave to stop being a monster and give Dominick a break.

Dave shouldn't back down, but he should put a time limit on his punishment, and if he doesn't want any repetitions of last night, he should also use this incident to teach Dom how to *reason morally*. This is the third step in respect-oriented discipline and it involves using questions to make a child step outside himself and look at how his misbehavior affects other people. Kids' natural egotism makes them world-class experts on instant gratification, but they're often a little slower when it comes to thinking how their actions can hurt or injure others, and using questions to help them make this key linkup does two important things.

First, it preserves self-respect and self-esteem, because realizing how he might have done harm gives a youngster a greater understanding of why you're mad at him and that makes him more willing to accept your anger. And, just as important, it also lessens the likelihood of repeat offenses, because from then on he'll begin to think about the way his misbehavior affects others.

I think you'll have a better understanding of the technique if I show you how Paul used it. He knew a couple of credit-card receipts weren't going to have much oral resonance to a seventeen-year-old like Colleen. So after their negotiation session, he asked Colleen how she'd feel if she knew that the $265 was supposed to have been part of the month's mortgage payment and now that it was spent, the payment couldn't be made.

Colleen thought about this for a minute, then said, "I'd feel terrible, Dad."

Paul's next question made her examine the consequences of this admission. He asked her, "Why would you feel bad, Colleen?" After another long pause, she replied, "Because if we couldn't pay the mortgage, we could lose our house."

Paul picked up on this reply by asking her, "Where would we live if we lost the house, Colleen?" And after hemming and hawing, Colleen admitted that if that happened, they might not have anyplace to live.

Now that Colleen's begun to reason morally, Paul can stop worrying about two things. First, he won't have to worry about Colleen's feelings being hurt. Before their talk, she might have been mad at Paul for being mad at her, but by knowing where her overspending could have put her family, she now understands why her dad was so upset. Another thing Paul won't have to worry about is what Colleen will say the next time someone asks her, "Do you want a drink, or a snort of coke?" or "Let's go to bed." One of the principal reasons kids say yes to these propositions is that they don't think, "What will happen if I say yes?" Their talk* has taught Colleen to ask herself this question. So she's not going to need Paul or another adult there to tell her why she should say no when one of these dumb ideas sails by her. She'll be better able to do that for herself.

I then showed Dave how to use questions to help Dom make these kinds of moral equations. It involved a role play where I played Dave and he played Dom.

---

* It should be pointed out that to foster a moral compass the techniques in this chapter have to be used consistently, over a period of years. It does not result from a single discipline encounter.

Father: Dominick, how would you feel if it'd been me in that police car and I'd been badly hurt in the crash?

Child: Pretty upset.

Father: How would you feel about the teenager who hit me?

Child: I'd be mad at him.

Father: Let's also say you knew that the crash hadn't been accidental—that you knew the teenager who hit me had been drinking.

Child: I'd be even madder at him.

Father: Why, son?

Child: It would make the accident seem stupider, Dad. You're a man with a family to support and this goofy kid decides to get drunk and plow into you. It wouldn't seem fair.

Father: You know, Dom, before we left the police station last night I talked to one of the cops who was in the car you hit last night. He told me he had a son about your age. Did you know that?

Child [surprised]: No, I didn't.

Father: How do you think he feels about you today, Dom?

Child: He'd probably like to strangle me.

Father: I don't know about that, but I'm pretty sure he wishes you'd stopped and thought about what you were doing last night. Okay, Dom?

Child: Okay, Dad.

"Do you see where I was leading Dominick with those questions?" I asked Dave.

"You were putting him in that other kid's shoes, weren't you?"

"Yes. Dom doesn't need anyone to tell him he behaved stupidly last night. He can figure that out for himself, but like Colleen and most other kids, he tends to think about his stupidity in terms of its consequences on *him*. It got you furious and him punished. A dialogue like the one we've just had forces Dominick to think about how that policeman's son would have felt if his dad had been killed, which Dom also can imagine easily, because he knows how he'd feel if you were killed. And once a youngster makes those kinds of connections he tends to be a lot more careful of how he behaves.

"Social concerns are just personal concerns writ large. So knowing how to put himself in another person's shoes will also give Dom a different and more personal understanding of epithets like 'nigger' and 'spic' and 'kike' and 'chink' because he'll be able to imagine how those names would make him feel. And a child who is able to make this kind of imaginative leap won't tolerate name calling or discrimination or selfish and greedy behavior in himself or in other people. And one thing America needs very badly now are more kids with these kinds of intolerances.

"Dave, you're smiling."

"I was thinking about Angelo, Ron. He used to use this kind of think-it-through trick with me all the time. I remember the time I hit Danny Moran in the eye with a snowball. He was real upset about it, because my snowball, which had a rock in it, came within an inch of knocking out poor Danny's eye. But Angelo didn't lose his temper. That was one of the things about my dad; most of the time he was like a popgun, but when I did something really bad or stupid, he'd get real quiet and calm. And that's how he was with this. After we took Danny home, he brought me back to our house, and said, 'Look, Davey, I want you to think about this question hard for exactly one minute: what woulda happened if you'd knocked Danny's eye out? Then when you're finished thinking about that, I want you to think about this: what would you have told Danny's mother if his eye had come out?' "

"I'm not surprised, Dave, our dads have been criticized a lot lately. But there were a couple of aspects of fathering that I think they understood better than we do. An example is *speaking out*, which is the fourth step in respect-oriented discipline.

"You and I and Beaver Cleaver knew that if our fathers didn't like certain behavior, we'd hear about it—and quickly. And we not only found that psychologically validating because it told us 'Dad cares'; we also found it useful. Those paternal yeses and nos were like a moral map of the world to us. We knew that if a behavior upset Dad enough to produce a protest, then it would probably upset a lot of other people. So we'd forget about the behavior.

"Our kids aren't so lucky. Not because we're less conscientious than our fathers. But because often we're so afraid of sounding authoritarian or too conservative if we say 'don't,' or 'no,' or 'I don't like that' that we tend to mute or stifle our criticisms in ways that leave a youngster thinking, 'Well, Dad never speaks up when I do this, so he mustn't mind it.' Emma Schwartz is a case in point.

"You didn't know her dad, Irv, Dave; he was in the project a few years before you. But his and Emma's story is a good example of what can happen when a father stifles his criticism out of fear of sounding too authoritative.

"One afternoon, Irv was sitting in his kitchen reading the paper when Emma, who was eleven at the time, and one of her friends walked in looking for something to eat. At first, Irv didn't pay much attention to the two kids. It was the year the Sox were in a tight pennant race and he was reading the sports pages. But then Emma, who was standing in front of the open refrigerator door, turned to her friend, and said, 'Oh, fuck, we're out of Jell-O.' "

"I'll bet that made him pay attention."

"It did, Dave. But just as Irv was about to speak up, he remembered how he used to feel when his dad delivered a lecture on vulgar language and he thought, 'Oh, God, if I say something, Emma's going to think I'm a nerd.'

"So he decided to let the incident pass. But like most dads who take this course, Irv came to dearly regret his decision to duck. Coming home from work one night, about six months later, he happened to pass two women at the Park Street MBTA Station. He remembered seeing both of them at a function at Emma's junior high, but evidently they didn't remember him because as he walked by them, one woman turned to the other and said, 'Honestly, that Schwartz child has a terrible mouth.'

"Irv made his second big mistake when he arrived home that night. He grabbed Emma by the back of the collar, when she came up to say hello to him in the hall, threw her against the wall and gave her the tongue-lashing of a lifetime."

"I came within an inch of doing that to Dominick last night. But then, I remembered what you'd told us about Self-expression."

"So what did you say to Dominick?"

"I told him, 'Dom, I know you're a good boy and I know that you didn't mean to upset me or your mother. But the fact is you have, pal, and I'm very, very mad at you.' "

"Good, Dave. While it's important not to let a mis-behavior—especially one like Dom's—go unchallenged, it's just as important to always correct a child in ways that preserve his self-respect. And your statement does that. You didn't blame Dominick by saying, 'You're a bad boy,' you framed his misbehavior in terms of its impact on you and Rose. And just as important, by beginning with 'I know you're a good boy' you showed Dom that, upset as you were last night, you didn't lose sight of his positive qual-ities. He's going to remember that thoughtfulness and it's going to make a difference in the way he deals with his friends and later on with his wife and with his own kids."

"I'm glad I did one thing right last night."

"I'm sure you did a lot of things right last night, Dave."

"And I'm sure you tell that to every father who comes in here with a problem, Ron."

"No, I don't. But I do tell every dad who comes in here to talk about morality what I told you earlier, Dave, giving a child a firm sense of right and wrong won't be enough; you also have to give him the independence of will and spirit to use it.

"There was a time when such independence wasn't so important because society and culture joined hands to sup-port paternal teachings about right and wrong and good and bad. So even if a child wavered, there were environ-mental props around to support him in weak moments. But these days, more often than not, society and culture are likely to conspire to undermine a man's teaching on things like greed, personal responsibility and sexual ethics.

"You can tell Dom, 'Greed is bad,' for example, but what's Dom going to think when he sees a Wall Street wheeler-dealer praised for his ingenuity in putting together a deal that made him a quick twenty million dollars and put three thousand other people out of work. And you could tell him, 'Because actions have consequences, you have to take responsibility for your behavior, Dom,' but what is Dom to think when other groups tell him that when bad things happen to good people, it's no one's fault, except maybe the federal government's for being too involved or not involved enough."

A father's worst enemy is often TV, because no matter what he tells his child about sexual morality, there's Jack on "Three's Company" telling him, "What matters most to a man is getting a pretty girl into bed." And no matter what you tell him about the futility and danger of violence, there're "Hunter" and "Magnum P.I." and a thousand other TV private eyes and cops telling him, "If a guy gives you a problem, do what I do, get a crowbar and bang him over the head."

Most men are different and better than Jack and Hunter and Magnum P.I. But ten-, twelve-, even seventeen-year-olds like Dominick Pullio have a harder time figuring that out. So when Nick Plazzo says, "Dom, this guy's giving me a hard time; let's do what Magnum P.I. does and get a crowbar" or "Dom, let's see if we can score with those girls in Arlington," it's hard for Dom to say, "No, Nick."

One way a parent can make it a little easier for his child is by steering him or her toward role models who thought so much of moral behavior they were willing to defy everyone around them to behave morally. Tom Paine, Abraham Lincoln, Joan of Arc, and Betty Friedan—all are terrific examples. If your daughter stood up and said, "Women count," at a moment when even most women didn't think they did, you'd be pretty proud of her. History and literature are full of people who had the courage to stand up and say the right thing in what they knew was the wrong time, and introducing kids to them teaches a child the importance of standing up for what he or she believes in.

You can also teach children the importance of independent thinking by making yourself an example of it. You know, a lot of their ideas are shaped by watching you, so if you use remarks like "I don't believe in statistical morality" or "I don't decide what's right and wrong by what other people do," you show your child that you're not afraid to stand apart from the pack and do your own thinking. Which means the next time your children hear those four magic words, "C'mon, everyone's doing it," instead of caving in they will think of your example and say, "Hey, I don't care who is doing it, I'm not doing it because I think it's wrong."

You can also make those words easier to say by showing a child how to think for himself. Will Meiser, a dad who was in the program a few years ago, was a master of this technique. Whenever his twelve-year-old, Gretchen, said, "But Dad, that's what all the kids think," Will would ask her, "But Gretch, what do *you* think?" And after talking over what she thought with her dad, often Gretchen would find that what she thought was a little different from what her friends thought. An example was Gretchen's thinking about Michael Jackson.

One afternoon she told Will her friends were going to a Michael Jackson concert and she was thinking of joining them.

Will had some reservations about this idea. At a time when teenage pregnancies are running at the rate of over a million a year, it occurred to him that Michael Jackson's suggestive onstage behavior might not make him an ideal influence on a suggestible twelve-year-old. But he didn't mention this concern when Gretchen brought up the concert. Instead, he simply said, "What do you think of Michael Jackson, Gretch?"

Gretchen tried to sidestep this question by saying, "All the kids think he's very sexy."

But Will decided the issue was too important to let her hide behind her friends, so he said: "Okay, you've told me what your friends think, now tell me what you think."

Gretchen hesitated for a moment, then said, "I think he's real cute, but all that hip shaking and stuff he does with the microphone is pretty gross."

"So," Will said, "it sounds like your feelings about Michael Jackson are a little different than your friends'. "

Gretchen also thought about this for a moment, then said, "Yes, Dad, I guess they are."

In the end, Gretchen didn't go to the concert. Will made that decision easier for her by showing her how to say no to her friends. Often kids say yes to things, not because they want to do them, but because they don't know how to say no and still look cool to the rest of the gang. So when Gretchen announced that she wasn't going, Will said to her, "Look, hon, I know you're concerned about what your friends will say, so let me show you how to put your no in a way that feels comfortable to you," and that's what he did.

Usually, kids equivocate when they're confronted by a group of opposite-minded friends, but when Gretchen was stopped in the cafeteria the next day by two of her friends, who asked, "Are you going, Gretch?" she had a reply ready. She said, "Seeing Michael Jackson may be worth thirty dollars to you guys, but I don't like him. I'm going to save my money until U2 comes to town." Dave's two kids could also benefit from this kind of coaching.

For example, Keri's boyfriend could use those four magic words, "C'mon everyone's doing it," to proposition her. Most kids who are put in this position equivocate because they can't think of an appropriate way to say no. But Keri won't, if Dave tells her beforehand, "Whenever anyone uses this line on you, tell them, 'Well, if everyone's doing it, you shouldn't have any trouble finding someone else to do it with you.'"

The same is true for Dominick. He'll find it much easier to say no to Nick Plazzo next time if Dave tells him the best way to handle Nick's invitations is to say, "No way, Nick—if you want to waste your body on booze, that's your business, but I'm not going to have any part of it."

One other way Dave can make it easier for Dominick to say no to Nick is to put Nick's popularity into perspective for Dom. Kids put a lot of value on qualities like good looks, athletic ability, and coolness. But no one's going to promote a forty-year-old Nick to senior vice president just because he's good-looking or super-cool or can run a 10K in thirty minutes. The qualities we value in people change as we get older.

We know this, but a seventeen-year-old like Dominick doesn't. He—and probably all his friends as well—imagine that Nick's coolness will continue to carry him from triumph to triumph. Pointing out to a child that values change, and with them the things we admire and respect in people, will help him put other kids into perspective. Saying no to the original Mr. Cool would be hard for anyone, but saying no to a fallible flesh-and-blood kid like himself is easy.

Before he left, I told Dave I had one more suggestion for him. It was about Dominick's chores.

"You have a dog, don't you?"

"Yeah, a weimaraner, Ron. His name's Hindenburg."

I had forgotten that Dave was a history buff.

"Who takes care of him, Dave?"

"Rose, mostly. She feeds and walks him; once in a while I help out."

"It would be a good idea if you made Hindenburg Dominick's responsibility from now on."

"He already has a lot of chores, Ron. He has to keep his room picked up, make his own lunch for school, and take out the garbage every morning. If anything's going to make him feel unfairly treated, wouldn't it be giving him one more chore to do?"

"Caring for Hindenburg doesn't have to be on top of, it can be instead of. You or Keri or Rose can take over one of Dom's other chores. Giving a child responsibility for another living thing is one of the best and subtlest ways a parent can foster moral development. Because no matter how skillfully you put your concerns about responsibility and fairness and kindness to others, there's still going to be an element of abstraction to them. Caring for Hindenburg is a way of putting some flesh and blood on those qualities for Dom. The love and gratitude Hindenburg will offer when he's walked or fed or brushed will make Dom feel good about himself and from that point it's only a matter of time before he discovers that caring for two-footed creatures will make him feel even better about himself. You can do the same thing with Keri."

"Ron, I've only got one dog."

"The responsibility doesn't have to be only to a dog, Dave. Chores that affect the well-being of everyone in the family will have the same moral effect on Keri. Knowing that you and Dom and Rose depend on her to help out with breakfast or to set the table at night will not only teach her about responsibility toward others, it will teach her about the rewards of responsibility."

As I finished talking, I noticed Dave looking down at his watch. "I know, I've got to go, too," I said. "I have a faculty meeting in ten minutes. Call me Wednesday. I want to know how you and Dominick make out in court."

"I will, Ron."

By this time, Dave had his coat on and was standing in my office doorway. "Oh," he said, "by the way, how are the guys in your new fathers' group?"

"Good, great, in fact."

"Great, Ron."

"Not as good as you guys, of course."

Dave winked.

"Just checking, Ron, just checking."

"I know, Dave, I know. Take care and don't forget to call me Wednesday."

7

How to Help a Child Become an Achiever

I don't know how Queen Elizabeth looks when she sees a new story about Princess Diana in the newspapers, but I imagine the expression that crosses the royal face at such moments isn't too different from the expression I saw cross Paul Cronin's one Saturday morning as he stared down at the threadbare Persian carpet that covered the small patch of floor under his chair.

"I came in for two reasons, Ron," Paul said as he eyed a bald spot in the rug, "one of which you may already know—Maureen and I are expecting again."

"No, I didn't know that, Paul. That's wonderful news. Congratulations."

"But the real reason I'm here is to talk to you about Tim, my fourteen-year-old. You met him at the Christmas party, didn't you?"

I remembered Maureen Cronin introducing me to a tall, handsome teenager with his father's dark hair and his grandfather's Ipana smile.

"Last Thursday, I had a pretty upsetting conversation with Mr. Kaufman, Tim's algebra teacher. At a basketball game a couple of weeks ago, he collared me at the candy stand and told me he wanted to have a conference. I thought we were going to talk about Tim's algebra. Tim nearly failed it last semester and he isn't doing too terrifically this semester either." Paul suddenly looked very serious.

"But Mr. Kaufman didn't want to talk about Tim's algebra?"

"He did and he didn't, Ron. He told me Tim's still doing poorly. But it was Tim's attitude he was worried about. Mr. Kaufman said Tim is an underachiever. Apparently he has all the earmarks of the syndrome. He has trouble sticking with problems, he blames other people for his failure, he's afraid to try and doesn't know how to plan."

"And what did you tell Mr. Kaufman, Paul?"

"I told him I'd had this conversation before. Last fall, it was with the school football coach, whom Tim was blaming for benching him. Tim's story was that the coach was doing it to spite him. But when I talked to the coach, he told me Tim was benched because he was always late for practice.

"About two weeks ago, I also had it with Norman Hensley, one of my neighbors. After the last snowstorm, Norman paid Tim fifteen dollars to clear his driveway. Tim quit halfway through, and two days later, Norman told me very nicely that if I didn't give him seven-fifty back, he was going to blow up my house. Mr. Kaufman says it's very common for characteristics like failure to follow through and blaming others to crop up in other areas of an underachiever's life. He also said underachievement isn't something a teacher can do much about. What do you think, Ron?"

"I'm afraid Mr. Kaufman's right, Paul. Most studies indicate that underachievement's roots lie in the home and how it promotes self-doubt. In plain English, underachievers aren't encouraged to believe in themselves and the fingerprint of that self-doubt appears on everything they say or do. That stick-to-itiveness Mr. Kaufman's so worried about is an example. Tim throws up his hands and quits when he gets a tough algebra problem because, in his heart of hearts, he doesn't believe he can solve it. And when you feel that way about yourself, you figure, 'Why even bother trying.'

"Tim's planning problems are another example of this negativism. At one point or another last fall, I'm sure it occurred to him that he ought to reschedule his day so he could get to football practice on time. But I'm also sure that his very next thought was, 'Forget it, even if I show up twenty minutes early, I'm still not going to win a starting position on the team.'

"Tim's habit of blaming others is also a reflection of his self-doubt. The sense of powerlessness this doubt generates makes kids very anxious, and one of the ways they deal with that anxiety is by blaming other people for their failures. I'll bet Tim makes a lot of excuses for himself, too. That's another common trait of underachievers."

"Mr. Kaufman says Tim's an A student in the excuse department."

"What else did Mr. Kaufman tell you, Paul?"

"That Tim has plenty of company. Apparently, underachievement is a leading cause of academic failure among American kids today."

Mr. Kaufman was right about that, too. The recent statistics on American students make pretty depressing reading. Nationwide high-school graduation rates are actually dropping, college entrance exam scores have remained flat for nearly a generation, and in a recent international comparison of math skills, American kids ranked twenty-first—two places ahead of Bolivia, eight behind South Korea, ten behind Singapore, nineteen behind Germany, and twenty places behind Japan.

When American parents see figures like these they think, "Our kids are being short-changed. We need more and better teachers and more and better school equipment." And we do need more of both. But most of all we need more students who arrive in the classroom already believing in themselves and their ability to excel. And as Mr. Kaufman said to Paul, that belief has to be nurtured in the home. In fact, not long ago it was estimated that if American parents were willing to spend an extra thirty minutes a day with their kids, it would do more to improve the quality of U.S. education than doubling the amount of money spent on schooling each year.

I told Paul if he was willing to give Tim those extra thirty minutes a day, I'd show him how to help Tim make himself an achiever.

"That's the real reason I came all the way in here on a snowy day, Ron."

"Good achievers and underachievers are mirror images of one another, Paul, just as all Tim's difficulties with stick-to-itiveness and blaming and making excuses and failing to plan flow from his low self-esteem. All the achiever's accomplishments in these and other areas flow from his high self-esteem—from his basic belief that he can do it."

"An achiever's a very self-confident kid, then?"

"An achiever's usually defined as a self-confident child who is *also* an effective plan maker and goal setter. These two qualities are inextricably linked, though, since a youngster won't bother making plans or setting goals unless he believes he can do what he sets out to do. The home must know how to—and, equally important, be willing to—provide the kinds of *competency-motivating* experiences that promote achiever behavior.

"Do you know what competency motivation means, Paul?"

"Wanting to do a job effectively."

"That's Webster's definition. But when psychologists use the term, they're usually referring to a concept that was developed by Professor Robert W. White of Harvard. He defined competence motivation as the *desire to influence or affect the environment* and from his work and that of other researchers, we know it is among the most elemental and profound of human drives.

"Every baby is born wanting to immediately begin influencing the people and things around him. A case in point is a German study I came across a few years ago. Its authors reported that their four-month-old subjects apparently got such a thrill out of being able to make the lights on a board wink on and off with their head movements that they developed the ability to learn and produce a complex series of movements for the opportunity to continue influencing their particular environment. The drive that kept these babies glued to their light boards is the same one that kept Darwin, Freud, Einstein, and Pasteur glued to their work."

Had Paul put a four-month-old Tim in with those other babies, he would have been just as eager. But in Tim's case, the drive to influence the environment never matured into the belief "I can influence the environment."

The two are quite different. Desire is a product of biology; belief is the product of three particular kinds of life experience.

Since Paul is about to be a dad again, I wanted to show him how the three experiences would apply to his new baby.

The first type of experience is known as *contingent responsive,* and it involves situations where a child is given the opportunity to make other people respond to her. This shows the child she has the capacity to influence their behavior. An example of such an experience for a baby would be smiling when she smiles at you, babbling when she babbles at you, pointing to your arm when she points to hers. All these things may sound very elementary. But the four- or five- or six-month-old who sees Dad responding to her gestures and maneuvers feels as though she's just made the sun and stars move.

The discovery of an unexpected talent or competency has the same effect on a child. And the best way to promote these kinds of discoveries is to *encourage exploration,* which is the second type of competency-motivating experience.

Exploration can be dangerous, noisy, and messy if a youngster is five months old. But you can offset the physical hazards of exploration by thoroughly baby-proofing your house. And while there's no known antidote to the noise and mess, you might keep this thought in mind as you watch your new baby rummage through the pots and pans under your sink: the freedom you've given her to explore will, at one point or another, result in an important discovery. She's going to find that she can make a sound when she bangs two pans together, and that realization will make her feel very masterful indeed, especially if you respond to her sound making and other feats with astonished admiration, which is the purest form of *parental respect*. This respect is the third kind of competence-promoting experience, in part because your admiration affirms the baby's pleasure in her triumph, but most of all because real astonished admiration tells a child, "Dad thinks you have such wisdom, such skill and fortitude, he believes nothing to be beyond you."

Let me tell you how changing the content of these three experiences would let Paul transform Tim's desire to influence the environment into a belief that he can influence it. For a thirteen- or fourteen-year-old, a special hobby or interest or project is the equivalent of a baby's smiling. It's a bid to influence the environment. The teenager is using the special interest as a vehicle to display his competence to himself and everyone else. And often, if he's successful, the effects of this success will show up later in the classroom.

Paul told me that Tim wanted to start a lawn-mowing business, and such a lawn-mowing service represents an opportunity to build Tim's self-confidence. And one way Paul can take advantage of it is by using his listening skills to provide Tim with contingent responsive experiences. What makes these situations so ego-boosting is that they show a child he has the ability to influence a key part of his environment—Dad. And that's what Paul would be showing Tim if the two of them had a conversation like this one:

> Tim: Gee, Dad, I'll bet lawn-mowing services make a lot of money.
>
> Paul: It sounds to me like you think there's big bucks in lawn mowing, Tim.

Tim: Yeah, Dad, I think there are for an adult. But
    do you think people would pay a kid like me
    as much as a grownup to mow their lawns?
Paul: You feel unsure of yourself, Tim?
Tim: I just don't know if I can do a good enough
    job, Dad. You know how I usually foul up.
Paul: I know you're worried because some of your
    other projects haven't succeeded, Tim, but
    don't forget, a lot have worked out, too. Re-
    member the great job you did repairing that
    rowboat on the lake last year? When you try,
    you usually do a good job.

This conversation is the equivalent of returning a baby's smile with a 1,000-watt one of your own. Paul's first
reflection lets Tim know he's gotten Paul interested in the
scheme. And with that assurance in mind, he's poured out
his worries about the competition, which gives Paul a
chance to tell him how much he believes in him and his
dream.

"Paul, you're biting your lip. That usually means you
have a question."

"Very observant, Ron."

"It's all those years of training. What do you want
to ask?"

"Right now, summer seems ten million miles away to
Tim. But one morning in May he is going to wake up, hear
the birds chirping in the trees, see the first blades of grass
sprouting up on our lawn, and then he's going to think,
'Uh-oh, I'm going to have to actually start a lawn-mowing
business.' How do I use the skills to give him another
1,000-watt smile when he comes to me on that morning,

as I'm sure he will, and says, 'Dad, I can't do it. I can't do it. I can't run a business. I'm still a kid'?"

"Just reflecting the fear in this statement is a form of contingent responsiveness, Paul. You're showing Tim he's influential enough to get you to listen while he pours out his heart. But beyond that, your reflection creates the kind of situation where another 1,000-watt smile will be possible. Let's play out this scenario, I'll show you what I mean.

"If I reflect Tim's fear by saying, 'It sounds to me like you're afraid you've gotten in over your head, son,' how would Tim respond?"

"He'd say, 'Dad, I am afraid. No one's going to trust their lawn to a fourteen-year-old.' "

"Well, that statement would give you a chance to flash Tim another 1,000-watt smile. He'd leave the conversation with his faith in himself restored if, after reflecting all his doubts up into the light, he heard you say, 'Tim, I've trusted my lawn to a fourteen-year-old and I know what a good job he does when he tries'; or alternatively, 'What people care about, Tim, isn't a person's age, but the job he does, and I know what a good job you do when you put your mind to it.' "

"Ron, the problem is you haven't actually talked to Tim. This is a boy who thinks the way to increase profit margins is to eliminate lawn baggers and rake up after yourself instead."

"Tim really wants to do that?"

"Yes."

"It's not a good idea, Paul."

"It's a terrible idea."

"Well, I certainly wouldn't tell him that. I might suggest his idea may not be as cost effective as he thinks. But if he insisted on trying his scheme I'd let him.

"For a teenager the freedom to make mistakes like eliminating baggers is the equivalent of opening the pots and pans cabinet to a baby; it's an *exploratory experience.* And in older children, Paul, exploratory experiences are the meeting place for two of the qualities which distinguish achievers. The chance to make an error and see the results when you correct it not only enhances a child's self-confidence, it also teaches him how to plan and set goals more effectively. But here's where the home, in the form of its willingness to provide competency-motivation experiences, enters the picture. In order to give a youngster the latitude to fall on his face, a dad has to believe enough in him to feel he'll be mature enough to learn from his mistakes and be responsible enough to apply what he learns next time—making better plans and setting more appropriate goals. .

"Do you have that kind of faith in Tim, Paul?"

"You're putting me into a corner, Ron. I believe in Tim enough to let him start his lawn business and even to eliminate the baggers if he wants. But do I believe in him enough to let him handle the finances and scheduling? No, my faith isn't blind. If Tim handles the money, all of it will end up going on clothes, records, and cheeseburgers; and if he does the scheduling, a lot of his jobs will be left half done. Tim, let me remind you, isn't the only one who will be affected by his project. Our neighbors are going to be his customers, and if he fouls up, it will reflect back on me and on Maureen and on our good name.

"I don't think that's an unreasonable position. We're talking about a fourteen- not a twenty-year-old, after all. Most fathers with kids Tim's age would tell you the same thing."

"I think many of them would, Paul, and I think we

may be seeing the results of all that paternal doubt and skepticism in those figures on academic achievement I quoted earlier. Putting restrictions on a child's freedom to make mistakes undermines his ability to learn how to make plans and set goals, because the restrictions say, in a not too subtle way, 'I don't believe in you.' And kids who don't feel believed in don't believe in themselves, and kids who don't believe in themselves do about as well as our kids have done lately in international competitions of science and math skills."

"Ron, this time Norman Hensley really will blow my house up if Tim walks away and leaves his lawn half done."

"I don't think you're putting restrictions on Tim because you're afraid of Norman Hensley or your good name, Paul; you're putting them on him because you're afraid of Tim's Ipana smile; it reminds you too much of your father's."

"What I do for Tim, I do for his own good. I don't want him growing up to be the kind of man who will leave his wife and child with eight dollars two days before Christmas, then disappear into Chelsea with his girlfriend."

"The hobby shop?"

"The hobby shop."

"I remember that story; it's touching."

"I have a lot more like it. But one thing I didn't come in here to do is talk about my father."

"I know you didn't, and I wouldn't have brought him up if I didn't feel he was relevant to Tim. A lot of his problems with self-esteem and confidence are linked to the fact that he knows you don't believe in and trust him. And most of your problems in these departments are linked to the fact that you keep getting Tim confused with Jack. Tim isn't your father. From what you've told me about the two of them, outside of an Ipana smile, they don't even sound alike."

"Tim's irresponsible, Ron. Jack was irresponsible."

"Irresponsibility is also a reflection of low self-esteem, Paul. The child doesn't have enough belief in himself to feel it's worthwhile to try to be responsible. Is Tim selfish enough to leave his wife and child with eight dollars, two days before Christmas?"

"Actually, Tim has a good heart."

"Is he a womanizer?"

"No."

"You said Jack lied a lot. Is Tim a liar?"

"No, usually not."

"Does he cheat?"

"No."

"Tim sounds pretty different to me. How about you, Paul? Paul, *Paul,* are you listening?"

"I'm thinking about what you've just said."

"Good, while you do that, let me tell you what's going to happen once you start seeing Tim and not your nightmares of him. All that wonderful potential of his you've talked about will begin looking even more wonderful. And as it does, you'll find your behavior changing. You'll start taking his interests and opinions more seriously, enjoy his triumphs more wholeheartedly, endure more inconveniences to get him to five a.m. hockey practices and Saturday-morning visits to the library, and you'll relax the reins and give him more freedom to explore his ideas and projects. These behaviors are the equivalent of clapping your hands in delight when the baby makes a sound with the pot, Paul, they're forms of *paternal respect* that say, 'I believe in you,' and you'll find that the more you believe in Tim, the higher his own estimation of himself climbs and, as I've said, one characteristic of an achiever is his high self-esteem.

"One word of advice though, Paul, don't be a mindless booster. Another characteristic of achievers is that, while they always try their best, they have a pretty good idea of what their best is, so they don't waste a lot of valuable time and energy pursuing impossible goals. And one of the things that makes them so discriminating is that they have dads who temper their high opinions with a measure of close observation. Children reveal a lot about their talents, interests, and abilities in their day-to-day behavior. And the achiever's dad picks up on these revelations and factors them into his high opinion. So while he always behaves in a way that conveys confidence and trust, it's a confidence and trust that are based on his knowledge of who the child is and not on the child's fantasies about himself.

"Paul, you're biting your lip again."

"What if Tim sets a really unrealistic goal?"

"Okay, let's assume that when you get home this afternoon he says, 'Dad, guess what, I figured out I can make five thousand dollars with the lawn service this summer.' You might, as with the baggers, gently suggest this is an unrealistic figure, but if Tim insists that five thousand dollars isn't unrealistic, tell him, 'If you feel that strongly, son, go for it.' One other characteristic of an achiever, Paul, is that he always sets his own goals."

"Ron, I don't think Tim can make five thousand dollars mowing lawns."

"I don't either, Paul. But we're not talking about what you and I think, we're talking about what Tim thinks, and what he needs now isn't your thinking but your trust and confidence. You need to believe in him enough to feel that at some point this summer he's going to say to himself, 'Oops, five thousand dollars was a crazy target to shoot for' or 'Oops, eliminating baggers to save money was a dumb idea.'

"These are the kinds of mistakes a child remembers and learns from, and if you give Tim the exploratory freedom to make them, you'll find that, as his store of memory and knowledge grows, a kind of chain reaction will set in. His mistakes will hone his skills to the point where his plans and goals begin paying off, and as they do, his confidence in himself and in his ability to make still bigger, better, and more ambitious plans and goals will grow, until finally Tim starts laying the kinds of plans and setting the kinds of goals that have him performing at the top of his ability. And I think most parents would agree that one very good definition of an achiever is a child who always performs at his best.

"Beth Cullen is a case in point. I think you'll find her story reassuring, Paul. Two and a half years ago, Beth had the same kinds of problems Tim has now. She was doing poorly in school, she had gotten cut from her cheerleading squad for missing games, and she had made her father, Joe, a nervous wreck, which is why he came to see me. Joe was sure Beth was on the road to ruin, and he was equally sure that the only thing that stood between her and a bad end was Joe Cullen.

"The more I listened to Joe, though, the more I thought his role in the Decline and Early Fall of Beth Cullen was a little different from the one he imagined himself playing. Joe was a loving and, in many ways, a wonderful dad, but he wasn't a particularly trusting or believing one; he'd always kept Beth on a very tight rein. And I suspected a lot of her problems with school and cheerleading were an expression of the low self-esteem a child has when the environment says, 'I don't trust or have confidence in you.'"

"Sounds familiar, Ron."

"Wait, Paul, you're going to love the end of Beth's story. I thought letting her take the part-time job she wanted would be a good way for the environment to give her a vote of confidence, which I told Joe, and which, after some nudging, I got him to agree to do. Normally it takes six or seven months for the learning curve on planning and goal-setting skills to kick in, and during that period Joe and I had some interesting discussions. Beth had proceeded to go from a bad to worse student, which is not abnormal, since often during the trial-and-error period, a child's performance dips a bit. But by the end of the sixth month, Beth knew she had become a competent enough planner and goal setter to balance her work and school responsibilities comfortably. That achievement made her feel so good about herself that she applied what she'd learned about planning and goal setting to her two problem subjects: history and geometry. When this produced positive results she planned and set goals for her college boards, and when those results also paid off, she applied herself to selecting a college. Last month Joe called to tell me Beth had gotten into Wellesley.

"Joe Cullen had done something very important. By letting Beth take that part-time job she wanted, he told her, 'I believe in you enough to think you'll know how to fit this job into your life.' Now that you've begun distinguishing Tim Cronin from Jack Cronin, I think you'll also find yourself sending this same validating message to Tim without even thinking about it. It'll just flow from you like music every time you look at that boy you love in your own imperfect way."

Aside from providing a nourishing environment, there are two other ways Paul can help Tim transform himself into an achiever. The first is by providing advice, guidance, and suggestions, if—and this is an important if—Tim asks him for them. If he's determined to prove to the world that eliminating baggers will revolutionize the lawn-mowing business, Paul should let him keep trying until he decides it won't. The lessons he learns from the failure will pay off the next year, when he's planning supplies for his window-washing business.

If, however, Tim does go to Paul in a week or two and says, "Dad, I don't know if dropping baggers was such a hot idea after all," Paul might tell him he thinks using baggers would probably save him a lot of time. Or, better still, he might say, "Look, Tim, why don't you try them for a few days and see what happens. If they save you a couple of hours, they'll be worth the extra few dollars. If they don't, you can drop them and go back to your old system."

The other way Paul can facilitate Tim's transformation into an achiever is by being there for him on those days when he comes home feeling brokenhearted because he's lost three customers or because he did foul up his scheduling and only had time to finish half of Norman Hensley's lawn.

Tim's probably going to make a lot of mistakes during the trial-and-error period, and some of them will leave Norman Hensley and Tim both feeling pretty blue. What he'll need and want at such moments is a father who believes in him enough to make him start believing in himself again. A lot of men think the way to do that is with praise. But when you've made a mistake that has you wondering, "How dumb can you get?," being told you're wonderful not only sounds unconvincing and tinny, it makes you feel misunderstood. You wonder, "Why is Dad telling me I'm a terrific person when I know a terrific person would've figured out a month ago that eliminating lawn baggers was a stupid idea?"

What you do want at such moments is someone there who not only knows how to listen while you talk about your pain and disappointment and anger at yourself for making such an obvious mistake, but who'll also help you bring all your feelings up into the light and who, after you're finished talking about them, will tell you how much he loves and believes in you. We call this unconditional warmth, and a good example of how it works in practice is the way John Uterhof handled Margery's disappointment when she got cut from her high school's production of *South Pacific*.

Canton High puts on a production of *South Pacific* every spring, and Margery had been dreaming about playing the Nurse Forbush role since her freshman year. So she felt pretty bad when she got eliminated in the first-round cut. Even when you're sixteen that kind of thing can make you feel you were pretty deluded about yourself, and Margery said as much to John, the night she told him about her elimination. "Imagine, Dad," she said, "I spent my freshman and sophomore years thinking I had the lead in *South Pacific* wrapped up, and I couldn't even get into the semifinals. How stupid can you get?"

John reflected this feeling back by saying, "You're pretty disappointed in yourself right now, aren't you, hon?" And when Margery replied, "God, Dad, who wouldn't be.

The whole world except me got into the semifinals," he reflected that feeling back by saying, "I know how important playing the Mary Martin part was to you, Margery. You must be feeling very low right now."

John didn't have to say much after that. Margery knew her dad understood this was an end-of-the-world situation for her. And knowing that, she felt free to pour out all her pain and anguish, which made her feel a little better. But what made her feel a whole lot better is the way that, at the end of their talk, John hugged her and told her how much she meant to him and how special he thought she was.

Unconditional warmth and the other things we've talked about here aren't a magical formula. But over time if you apply them with care, diligence, and love, I think you'll help a child be who he wants to be and they'll also help you.

They'll help the child, because they'll give him the confidence and skills he needs to realize all that wonderful potential of his, and they'll help Dad, because as the child becomes more confident, he'll find himself spending less and less time having talks with people like Mr. Kaufman, Norman Hensley, the football coach, and me.

8
Fathers and Sons, Fathers and Daughters

"Is he supposed to be Rambo or GI Joe, John? I can never tell whether my nephew's being one or the other. He gets very insulted."

"It's the headbands, Ron."

"What about the headbands, John?"

"They're why you get GI Joe and Rambo confused. They both wear headbands."

"I see."

(Rambo's and GI Joe's headgear was a new problem for me. I need another minute to think.)

"Well, John, how do you tell Eric Rambo from Eric GI Joe?"

"Weapons. When Eric's Rambo, he has an Uzi submachine gun and a Walther PPK pistol; when he's GI Joe he has a Browning semiautomatic and a Smith and Wesson .45."

"I'm glad to hear Joe buys American."

The pictures John Uterhof had spread out on my desk

were taken the previous Halloween, and if you ignored the old Victorian house in the background, you could see why John felt the nine-year-old in them might be a visitor from one of his worst dreams. Eric Uterhof has his father's height and his powerful shoulders, and with camouflage paint smeared across his face and an alarmingly authentic-looking Uzi submachine gun strapped across his chest, Eric looked real and deadly enough to embody everything his sweet, earnest, pacific-minded, Volvo-owning father abhors.

John, being John, was making an effort to be fair-minded and considerate about his son's interests. But he was also worried about what the photos said about Eric's state of mind. Which is why he was sitting in my office on this springlike late-winter day wearing a frown nearly as big as the Uzi strapped on Eric's chest.

"I remember enough of my college psychology to know that, clinically speaking, identification with powerful masculine figures isn't abnormal for a boy," John said as he reached over and began collecting the photos from my desk. "But a few weeks ago, I saw a photo of a Palestinian boy about Eric's age in *Time*, with a real Uzi in his hands, and I thought, clinically speaking, his behavior wouldn't be considered abnormal either."

"Which made you wonder about the wisdom of people who speak clinically?"

"It was a frightening photo, Ron."

"I know, John, I saw it too. The boy was staring into the camera as if he thought he was all the Masters of the Universe rolled into one. But Boston isn't Beirut and Eric isn't growing up in a society which makes its nine- and ten-year-olds look that way, thank God. He's just a boy trying on a fantasy a couple of sizes too big for him, which is normal, John, and will pass as he matures and his interests change."

"I understand that," John said as he carefully put the last of the photos in his wallet. "And I also understand how important it is for a parent to allow his child the freedom to explore his fantasies."

"But?"

"But I don't want Eric to grow up with the idea that a submachine gun can be equated with masculinity. That notion has been the source of enough needless tragedy in the world. Do you think I'm unfairly imposing my fears on Eric?"

"John, don't apologize for hating that equation. I wouldn't want my son thinking a submachine gun represents masculinity either. It's a pernicious idea and, for a youngster like Eric who's going to come of age in a society where men will be expected to conform to a more enlightened code of masculine behavior, it's also a dysfunctional one. By the time Eric's thirty, he and other men will be expected to know what characters like Michael Kramer (Dustin Hoffman in *Kramer vs. Kramer*) and Cliff Huxtable (Bill Cosby) already seem to know: how to exude strength without chest thumping or gun waving and how to have authority without being unresponsive or emotionally inexpressive.

"The Rambos and GI Joes of the world are passing into a happy and well-deserved obsolescence, John. And we're all—men and women—going to be better people for their passing."

John nodded. "Ron, couldn't you fairly say the same thing about women? It seems to me the codes of female behavior are changing just as quickly."

"I agree. Given the way women's roles and aspirations are changing, by the time your Margery is in her mid-twenties, the June Cleaver model of femininity will be just as dysfunctional as the chest-thumping model of masculinity will be for men of Eric's generation."

The dependency and passivity of the June Cleaver model will also constitute a personal and professional liability in a society that expects its women to be assertive and self-reliant, especially in the workplace.

Probably the greatest single challenge facing fathers today is preparing their kids for this New Egalitarian Age.

What makes it a special challenge for dads is that it's the man who plays the paramount role in shaping a child's ideas about male and female behavior. This doesn't mean women are only spectators in the gender-role identification process. But their contribution to the process is largely made through example; women model traits and behaviors, but research shows that men actively shape their responses to a child's gender. And it also shows, even today, that most paternal behavior is shaped to fit the traditional notions of masculinity and femininity, which produce June Cleavers and Rambos.

Conventional thinking, for example, holds that males are supposed to be physically strong, emotionally tough, and slightly roguish. And observational studies show that even with infant sons, a man will comfort, play, and talk in ways that fit these preconceptions. A dad, for instance, is much quicker to engage in roughhousing and other forms of physical play (toughness), and much more likely to allow exploratory freedom. I have also observed that in conversations with an infant son a father is much quicker to drop his voice an octave or two and use a rakish form of endearment like "you little devil" or "you little hellfire."

If infant sons are treated like miniature Indiana Joneses, infant girls are treated as if they were the living embodiment of the sweet, delicate, vulnerable confection described, in the old nursery rhyme, as "sugar and spice and everything nice." During play, baby girls get more paternal smiles and soft vocalizations (sweetness), and they are held as if every little girl came with user's instructions that warned, "Handle With Care."

Certain traditional people in New Guinea have an interesting belief. They think a child born with an umbilical cord around its neck is destined to become a great artist, and—lo and behold—all of the tribe's great artists have been born with umbilical cords around their necks. Paternal behaviors have the same element of self-fulfilling prophecy about them. Baby boys aren't innately stronger, emotionally or physically, than baby girls, just as the girls aren't innately more coquettish or social than the boys. But Dad's treating each sex as if these differences were real tends to make them real ten or fifteen years later.

A case in point is a study some Boston University colleagues and I did several years ago on dependency, a trait most men believe to be innately female. While our data showed it isn't, they also showed that men acted on this belief in a way that ended up fostering a daughter's dependency. An example is the way many of our test fathers acted in problem-solving situations. Instead of encouraging a stumped daughter to come up with an answer of her own—a strategy we know fosters independent thinking—these fathers intervened with a solution at the first sign of trouble.

We know from other problem-solving studies that when the stumped child is a boy a father won't intervene. He'll encourage a son and provide helpful hints, but he'll make the boy provide the answer. In other words, the dad will be supportive in a way that encourages independence. But because of the way men view daughters, a little girl is helped in a way that says to her, "You're out of your depth. You need a man's help." And twenty or thirty years later, the adult woman will remember Dad's words when she has a marketing campaign to plan or a trial brief to prepare. Which means instead of thinking, "I can do it," she's going to think, "I can't," and reach out for the nearest available male help. So the cycle of dependency will repeat itself once more, except this time it will repeat itself in a society that expects, as a matter of course, that women will be competent at tasks like planning marketing campaigns and trial briefs.

In the father-son relationship, the paternal prophecy-making process is geared to produce a strong, fearless, emotionally inexpressive, sports-loving twelve-year-old boy, and because of the special connection between fathers and sons, with boys the process tends to be more relentless and unforgiving. A father, for example, often won't say anything to a three-year-old daughter caught with big brother's Construx set, but studies show that a three-year-old son caught with big sister's Barbie usually will be rebuked and Barbie quickly removed from his arms. The data also show that while little girls are given some latitude to indulge in unfeminine behaviors, a little boy who displays "unmasculine" traits can expect to be treated the way I saw one of my six-year-old neighbors treated recently.

I think you'd find this six-year-old's dad, Mike, a generally enlightened and thoughtful man. But as with a lot of men today, Mike's anxiety to produce that fearless, strong, sports-loving twelve-year-old sometimes leads him to impose behavioral standards that shouldn't be imposed on a six-year-old boy. And the scene I witnessed was a case in point.

Arriving home from work one night, I saw Mike, who was also coming home, hop out of his car and call to his kids, who rushed out of the back yard to greet him. The first to reach him were his nine-year-old twins, and for their fleet-footedness Abby and Denise each got a big paternal hug and kiss. But when six-year-old Tommy, who was bringing up the rear, arrived and opened his arms for a hug, Mike suddenly stuck out his hand and said very seriously, "Hugging's for girls, Tommy, we men always shake hands."

Twenty-five years from now, Tommy will remember his dad's words when his six-year-old son rushes up to hug him and he'll also stick out his hand. Except Tommy's going to stand out in a society that recognizes that six-year-old boys need as much hugging and kissing as six-year-old girls. And so Tommy's outstretched hand will make him stand out not only to his wife and to passersby like me, but to his six-year-old, who'll wonder why his dad is the only one on the block who doesn't hug and kiss and also wonder what that reticence says about Dad's feeling toward him.

John was squirming in his chair—a behavior that, over the months, I'd learned to recognize as a sign of disagreement.

"John, has something I've said upset you?"

"I'm unhappy with the toy studies you mentioned, Ron."

"Why?"

John cleared his throat and steeled himself for our first disagreement. "I've tried to be as physically affectionate with Eric as I've been with Margery. But I don't understand why you feel the behavior of the men in those studies is developmentally unsound. I wouldn't like a four-year-old Eric playing with Barbie any more than I like a nine-year-old Eric playing with an Uzi."

"John," I said, "you're doing what a lot of dads do: you're looking at Barbie through your eyes, not those of a four-year-old Eric who would see her the way he sees his He-Man sword, his racing cars, and his other toys—as just another tool for exploring and expressing his different sides.* The sword gives him a tool to explore his aggression, the car his mechanical aptitudes, and Barbie or her equivalent in a stuffed animal his nurturing impulses. All men have these, and when a father interferes with their development by taking away the doll or the stuffed animal but leaving the He-Man sword or the racing car, he's not only blocking his four-year-old's normal exploration, he's also saying, 'Dad approves of aggression but not of tenderness.' And that, John, is another message that already has caused the world enough needless tragedy.

"You've given Margery and Eric the freedom to follow their interests and impulses in other areas of their lives, and that's also the appropriate policy to adopt with sex-role identification. Traits like self-reliance, aggressiveness, and nurturance occur with about equal frequency in both sexes, and the man who realizes this and is able to push aside his preconceptions is likely to have the all-boy and

---

* A ten-, eleven-, or twelve-year-old boy who continues to show a preference for dolls and other female toys and objects is behaving abnormally for a male of his age, and very likely does need some form of professional assessment and guidance. However, I personally have doubts about the efficacy and wisdom of therapy that is aimed at transforming an effeminate child into a "normal boy." A parent should guide and shape, but he should also accept who his child is, and if he happens to be different, understand and come to terms with those differences.

all-girl twelve-year-old he wants, and something even more important: a son who knows how to be sensitive and caring and masculine all at once and a daughter who knows how to be independent, self-reliant, and assertive, yet feminine, too.

"I know these are the traits you want for Eric and Margery, John, but fostering them will require you to step outside of your conditioning and upbringing, and that isn't easy, even for a father as sensitive as you. Traditional notions of masculinity and femininity are so deeply ingrained in our culture that even fathers who are aware of their hazards often end up being trapped by them anyway. My study is an object lesson. Our pretest assessments indicated that a lot of our participating fathers wanted to foster independence and self-reliance in their daughters, but when these men went into the test situation, their conditioning won out and they ended up behaving like the most traditional dads."

"How does a man escape the influence of his conditioning then, Ron?"

"Self-awareness is the key, John. But given the subtlety and persuasiveness of sex stereotyping, a man needs a special form of Self-awareness. If you ask me to give it a name, I'd call it consciousness raising, and if you ask me to define its constituent parts, I'd say that while it includes many of the techniques you learned in the program, it also involves two other forms of Self-awareness we didn't talk about. The first is an awareness of the recent research on biologically based sex differences. You know when a dad gives a daughter the answer to a problem or refuses to hug his son, he's usually responding to what he thinks are the different needs and drives of each sex. But the new research shows that, outside of the obvious ones, most of the differences between males and females are really relatively marginal. And often, just an awareness of that marginality will make a man's behavior more even-handed and egalitarian."

Much of the overprotectiveness dads display toward daughters is based on the belief that females are biologically more vulnerable to anxieties and fears. But there's no scientific evidence to support this contention.

Studies of other supposedly unique male and female traits like sociability, motivation, and assertiveness also have failed to find profound innate differences between the sexes. There's also growing evidence that mathematics, which has long been thought to be a male preserve, may be a more sex-blind talent than we'd imagined. A recent survey of high-school seniors in twenty countries found no significant differences in the math ability among boys and girls.

Even in areas where sex-linked differences have been discovered, the differences have to be put into perspective. On average, for example, we know that males are bigger, stronger, and have the edge in visual-spatial abilities like depth perception, while women tend to have superior verbal facility. But we also know there are quite literally tens of millions of boys and girls who fall outside these averages. Which means that the man who allows the averages to color his perceptions of his child may miss his child's specialness; he may also miss it if that child turns out to have the potential to be a Madame Curie or Margaret Thatcher or Truman Capote or has some other quality which puts him or her outside the averages.

On the office wall almost directly above where John was sitting is a photo of my daughter Caren and me, which was taken on the cold November day in 1965 Caren turned three months old. I suppose in most ways, it isn't any different from the photos of fathers and infants you see hanging on the walls of thousands of other offices. Caren looks, as baby girls in such pictures do, transcendentally lovely, and as with most young fathers, my twenty-three-year-old chest is puffed out to the size of the Astrodome. But there's also a special story behind the picture and I mentioned it to John as a way of making a point about the second form of Self-awareness that a man needs in order to foster the qualities and traits that will make his boy or girl at home in twenty-first-century America.

It's an awareness of the signals and messages the environment—and primarily the environment in the form of Dad's behavior—sends to the child, and what connects it to the picture on my office wall is that just before it was taken my wife and I realized that our three-month-old daughter was already shaping her responses to our distinctly male and female cues. Like most fathers' behavior, mine with Caren was usually playful, and I told my wife that Caren seemed to notice it and was reacting to me accordingly. Whenever I took her in my arms, she'd immediately perk up as if to say, "Oh, Dad, it's you, that must mean we're going to play." My wife laughed and said Caren did the same thing with her, except in her case, Caren quieted as if to say, "Oh, Mom, it's you, that must mean I'm going to get some gentle rocking and cooing."

"Do you know what the moral of my story is?" I asked John after I'd finished it.

"Yes, I think I do, Ron. Even with an infant a father should be aware that he's already shaping his child's ideas about male and female behavior."

"John, they are going to give you my job."

John glowed.

"Now, why don't you tell me how that moral is linked to the second form of Self-awareness."

"A man should know which of his cues send egalitarian messages to his baby?"

"Right, and in the first few months of life, one cue that does that is becoming involved with nursing chores like bathing and feeding and dressing."

Most of us grow up dividing the world into female nurturers and male buddies, and it's because the traditional division of labor in infancy encourages us to begin making that distinction even before we know we're making it. Feeding a baby is a way for Dad to show the baby that qualities like playfulness and tenderness are not the exclusive domain of either sex.

Colors also can send a message to even a very young child, and avoiding the traditional blue for boys and pink for girls is another way a man can keep his infant from prematurely dividing the world. I don't think, for example, that any father today wants his daughter growing up thinking of herself as the sweet confection described in the sugar-and-spice rhyme. But as Letty Cottin Pogrebin notes in her book, *Growing Up Free*, that is the message every shade of pink sends to a baby girl. Petal pink stands for delicacy, cotton pink for sweetness, and baby pink for tenderness, vulnerability, and helplessness. Pink also stands for something else, Ms. Pogrebin notes, and she points to the lyrics of "Soliloquy," one of the songs from the Rodgers and Hammerstein musical *Carousel*, to demonstrate it. It goes:

My little girl, pink and white as peaches and cream is she,

My little girl is half again as bright as girls are meant to be!

And as for baby blue, Ms. Pogrebin makes an equally telling case against it. She thinks blue subtly encourages traits like coldness and no-nonsense practicality. But her point isn't that a pair of pink or blue pj's will irretrievably warp the mind of the nine-month-old who's put inside them. She's simply saying—and justifiably, I think—that when environmental cues, like clothing and furniture and color, conform to our conventional notions of masculinity and femininity, they're very likely to produce a boy or girl with a very conventional idea of who men and women are and how they should behave.

Since toys are the key environmental cue for three-, four-, five-, and six-year-olds, boys who are surrounded by nothing but hypermuscular figures like He-Man and Lion-O, Lord of the Thundercats, and girls who are surrounded by nothing but Rainbow Brites and Sweet Secrets are likely to have the same narrow-minded view of the sexes.

As with color, this doesn't mean that a Batman or a Captain Power or a Barbie on the toy shelf will permanently distort a child's thinking. But it does mean the environment, in the form of Dad, should try to balance his cues by providing a broad enough mix of toys to allow his son to express his tenderness and nurturing impulses and his daughter her assertiveness.

A toy-buying father will always ask himself, "Is my child going to like this?" But an equally relevant question in such circumstances is "What cues am I sending with this toy?"

In a different form, this question also becomes relevant to a lot of other seemingly commonplace situations.

For example, a dad's reaction to dirt usually is shaped by the sex of the child under it. The boy will get a dressing down, but the twinkle in the scolding dad's eye will tell him, "Dad thinks you're a real boy." Often, the only thing a dirt-covered little girl will see in Dad's eye is a big "Ugh!" Dirtiness is an equal-opportunity condition and it should be treated that way. If required, an impartial scolding should be administered and then the youngster should be directed to the showers.

Bedtimes are another occasion where the question "What cues am I sending?" becomes relevant. I know most men don't think of this as a potentially sexist situation. But it can be and, in this case, the victim is usually a son. Dad will be full of hugs and kisses if he's saying goodnight to a daughter. But men tend to put their sons to bed the way my friend Mike greeted his son, Tommy. There'll be some hugs and kisses, but often those hugs and kisses are offered in the kind of brisk, businesslike fashion that says "Dad's not comfortable behaving this way, and if you're a real boy, you won't be, either."

In the late-preteen and teen years, the question "What cues am I sending?" becomes especially relevant to the issues of money. Put yourself in the position of the eleven-year-old girl whose dad spends forty dollars on her thirteen-year-old brother's baseball glove and ten dollars on hers, and you'll see what I mean. What kind of message would that dad's behavior send you?

I asked John to put himself in the shoes of a sixteen-year-old like Margery who sees her father initiating her fourteen-year-old brother into the mysteries of checking accounts and money market funds, but not her, because he doesn't consider it something a girl needs to understand.

"You know, financial knowledge is going to be vitally

important for women of Margery's generation, John. By the turn of the century, I expect that almost every American woman will have an independent income, in the form of a salary check, and a great many of them will be shouldering enormous financial responsibilities. Sending a daughter into this world as a financial illiterate is as disadvantageous to her as sending her into it as a computer illiterate. Her ignorance will affect her ability to function successfully and effectively. Are you doing anything to introduce Margery to the financial facts of life?"

"She's asked me about opening a checking account a few times."

"And?"

"And I've told her I thought sixteen was a little young to be thinking about checking accounts."

"Suppose, instead, Margery had said, 'Dad, I don't feel like going to school today.' What would you think then?"

"What any man who's been through the program would think, Ron. Margery had a hidden thought or feeling she wanted some assistance in identifying."

"What makes you think she wasn't saying that when she asked about the checking account?"

"The thought never occurred to me, Ron."

"John, that unthought thought is why the third kind of Self-awareness a man needs to exercise is an awareness of how his preconceptions can get in the way of his ability to use the program's skills. We call this phenomenon gender-induced amnesia, and we see it quite a bit at the project. When sex-typed behavior becomes an issue or problem, the dad suddenly forgets everything he's learned about Self-expression, Understanding Hidden Messages, and Negotiation.

One such attack of gender-induced amnesia happened during a role play we did to help Sam Aberjanassi use Self-expression to handle his four-year-old, Denisa's, protests about day care. Sam had said, "Denisa, I know you wish Mommy and I could stay home with you all the time, and I know sometimes you feel a little anxious at the center, but in order to buy all the things we need, Mommy and I both have to work. Besides, we like the center and we like Mrs. Carson [the center's director]. We know that she cares about you almost as much as we do."

But right after he showed us how sensitive he could be in his handling of Denisa, gender-induced amnesia struck. I had asked him to imagine that he had just caught Denisa climbing a tree, and his response had been: "Denisa, get down from that tree. Little girls aren't supposed to climb trees."

Something very similar happened not long ago to Greg Angstrom, a father who's in my spring group. Greg has a teenage son and daughter and, like a lot of men with adolescents, he has some concerns about their sexual conduct. I built a role play around those concerns and asked Greg how he'd use Self-expression to talk to his kids about their sexual behavior.

With Hildy, his fifteen-year-old, Greg was masterful. He said, "Hildy, you're in a very exciting period of your life. But adolescence is also a very sensitive time for a young woman. She wants to be thought attractive and desirable by the opposite sex, and while that's perfectly normal, sometimes that wish can lead her to make foolish choices. So I'd like you to keep a couple of things in mind." This statement acknowledged Hildy's concerns about herself as a soon-to-be-adult and about her desire to be popular with boys. And most important of all, it made the advice Greg then proceeded to give her seem like a natural and logical outgrowth of Hildy's concerns for herself.

With his seventeen-year-old, Harry, however, Greg suffered an acute attack of gender-induced amnesia. In fairness, in many ways, this is a tougher situation for a man to handle. Our culture winks at sexual roguishness in males, especially young males. So when a sixteen- or seventeen-year-old boy says, "C'mon, Dad, you did the same thing when you were my age" or "Hey, can I help it if I'm a normal healthy boy?" a father—even a father who has learned how to state his concerns in a straight-forward manly way—is in a tough position. He doesn't want his son thinking sex is a game or a form of machismo; on the other hand, a part of him doesn't want his son thinking, "Dad's such a wimp."

I wanted to see if Greg would be able to overcome these impulses. At first Greg's mature paternal side seemed to have the upper hand. He ignored the sexual swaggering of the dad who was playing Harry and proceeded much the way he had with Hildy. But the other dad knew which buttons to press and when the right time came, he pressed them hard by saying, "Give me a break, Dad, can I help it if I drive the girls crazy?" As he listened to these words, you could almost hear Greg thinking, "Should I or shouldn't I correct him?"

And Greg decided he shouldn't, or probably more accurately, he couldn't bring himself to. So from that point on, the role play descended into a sanitized version of a locker-room talk, with Greg playing the appreciative audience, and the dad, who was Harry, the sexual raconteur and warrior. It was both a funny and sad moment.

Jack Duffy, another program dad, came down with a case of gender-induced amnesia very similar to John's a few years ago when his son, Sean, announced he wanted to enter a line of work his father didn't think entirely appropriate for a twelve-year-old boy—baby-sitting. The hidden feeling behind Sean Duffy's repeated attempts to get his dad to sit down and talk about the service was the very healthy adolescent's desire to begin assuming a little more responsibility. But Jack's case of amnesia was so severe that he couldn't hear this until he was administered shock therapy in the form of that ever effective paternal remedy—guilt.

One night the father of one of Sean's friends, who's a vice president at Prime Computer, called to say Sean wanted to talk to him about the sitting service. The man told Jack he'd be happy to give Sean all the time he wanted, but he said, "I thought I ought to check with you first—I know how I'd feel if my boy went to another father on a thing like this."

At breakfast the next morning, a very surprised and pleased Sean suddenly discovered that his father couldn't hear enough about the sitting service. And by the time the meal was over, Sean was thinking how lucky he was to have such an understanding and helpful dad. And Jack was thinking how lucky he was to have a son who had so much initiative and responsibility that he was starting his own business.

"John, if you stop and reflect the next time Margery asks you about the checking account, I think you'll find she's also telling you, 'Dad, I think it's time for me to begin exercising a little responsibility and initiative.' And please don't feel guilty. You have a wonderful relationship with Margery. One little oversight won't affect it. And to reduce the risk of any repetitions let me tell you how to identify the signs of gender-induced amnesia."

One common sign is a pattern of gender-specific problem emotions. These are feelings a man can express freely to one sex but not the other. And in the case of fathers and daughters, the most common of them, usually, is anger—which, for cultural reasons, men find relatively easy to express to boys, but very hard to express to girls. In the case of fathers and sons, the most common is fear of authoritarian behavior, and it's usually linked to the dad's worry that his restrictions may inhibit his son's self-reliance.

The man who has trouble dealing with out-of-gender messages like female expressions of assertiveness and independence or male expressions of fear or tenderness also is very likely suffering from a form of gender-induced amnesia. And in both cases, the best remedy is Self-awareness in the form of some honest self-scrutiny where the dad sits down and tries to get in touch with the things in his background, values, or experience that are making it hard for him to hear messages or behave in ways that don't conform to our traditional notions of male and female behavior.

Part III

The New American Family

How the skills help in coping with divorce, stepfathering, and the working-parent family

9
What to Tell Kids About a Divorce

The coffee shop on Columbus Avenue that George Phelan had suggested was as bleak and deserted as the Sunday morning streets outside. The only customer was George, who was sitting alone in a booth by the window with a big black cloud over him and an uneaten English muffin on the table.

"Good morning, George."

George looked up, startled. "Oh, Ron. 'Morning. Sorry about this place. I couldn't think of anywhere else to meet. I'm homeless at the moment."

"Where did you stay last night?"

"The Y on Huntington Avenue."

"Oh, God. Was it bad?"

George smiled faintly. "It looked a little like Room 301, actually."

I'd known for some time that the Phelans' marriage was in trouble. At his intake interview the previous September, George had hinted at marital problems. And he'd brought them up directly one night in late November when the two of us found ourselves walking out to the parking lot together after a meeting. I had offered to give him the name of a marriage counselor, but he had declined.

"Have you told Billy and Megan yet?" I asked after the waitress brought my coffee.

George shook his head. "Not officially. They've been at their grandmother's all week. Elizabeth packed them off last Sunday after the two of us got into a screaming match at dinner. They know something's up, though. All I get out of Billy anymore is yes and no and uh-huh; and Megan—poor Megan. The other night I was sitting on the bed laying out my ties when she came in and put her arms around me. She didn't say anything and I didn't either, we just hugged one another like we were the last two people in the world."

"Megan knows, then."

"Megan knows."

"But you're wondering how to get her and Billy through the divorce without any permanent scars?"

George nodded. "That's why I wanted to talk to you. Be my Pat O'Brien."

The first thing George needed to know was that a lot of children aren't permanently scarred by divorce. One out of every three kids today lives through a divorce; and 55 to 60 percent of them emerge from the experience pretty much intact.

"I know that still leaves the odds facing Billy and Megan pretty high. But there's a lot that you and Elizabeth can do to help them beat those odds; though, for a while, it won't seem that way.

"For the first year or so, the two of you are going to

find yourselves facing what looks like an unbreachable wall of sadness, anger, and resentment. It might help to know that most divorced parents do."

Kids see the collapse of a marriage as a parental problem that has been allowed to intrude into their own lives. Mom and Dad are supposed to know better, and a five- or ten-year-old doesn't know yet how complicated human relationships are. To them, a divorce is like a rule change in the middle of the game. After playing by contract-bridge rules all their lives, suddenly they're told, "We're playing by Solitaire rules now." Confusion, betrayal, anger, and hurt are all normal and common in this situation, but, typically, boys and girls express these feelings differently.

Girls are much more likely to internalize their anger and pain, so Megan probably will express her distress at the divorce in long, mournful silences and frequent crying jags. Over the next year, I told George, there were going to be lots of tearful scenes with Megan.

"What about Billy, Ron?"

"In some ways, the divorce will be even harder on him. Megan will still have an adult female in the house to look to when she wonders, 'How should I behave?' or 'What should I think?' With you gone, Billy won't, and that loss will produce a lot of anger and aggressive behavior that could create some serious problems for Elizabeth and for you.

"Billy also has some things working in his favor, though, the most important of which is his age. Children who face the twin stresses of divorce and the transition to adolescence are in the high-risk group. However, by the mid-teen years, a youngster's usually developed some pretty sophisticated coping mechanisms. And the self-absorption of adolescence offers its own protection. For the next few years, Billy will be so preoccupied with himself, he's not going to have that much time for you and Elizabeth and your problems."

"Megan's only eight."

"And that may work against her, George. For an eight-year-old, Mom and Dad are still the sun, moon, and stars. So their divorce is like the heavens suddenly upending. It's shocking and enormously disorienting.

"Remember, though, risk factors like age and sex just calculate probabilities; they tell us what might happen to a child of divorce in a given set of circumstances. What will actually happen to Megan and Billy depends on you and Elizabeth. There are three areas that have an enormous influence on a child's post-divorce recovery. And if you look at the research, you'll find that the kids who put the normal pain and anger of a divorce behind them after the first year are the ones whose parents have learned to cooperate in these three areas.

"I realize working together won't be easy for you and Elizabeth, George. Divorce produces a lot of ugly feelings in adults, too. But if you and she want Billy and Megan to have this experience largely behind them by this time next year, you're both going to have to learn how to set aside your differences when you find yourselves in one of these three areas."

George took a bite of his English muffin. "What are they, Ron?"

"The first is working together to *allay the normal fears and anxieties* stirred by a divorce. You've got an opportunity to start doing that with the announcement. You said you haven't told the kids yet?"

"No, my sainted spouse is going to do it tomorrow night."

"Are you going to be there, George?"

"I'm not sure I'm that brave. It's not going to be pleasant."

"I know it isn't. But I think it would be a good idea if you were there for the announcement. News of a divorce stirs three immediate concerns in children. They wonder if they're responsible for the breakup, how it's going to affect their own little world, and what will happen to Dad. Being there is a way of ensuring that these fears are properly addressed. The words you choose should be your own, but can I give you some advice, George?

"I've talked to a lot of divorced dads and I think you might benefit from their experience. Most of them have found that the announcement itself usually is so traumatic and overwhelming that vague reassurances like 'Everything's going to be all right, kids' don't sink in. You need to address each fear directly and individually. Have you and Elizabeth talked about living arrangements yet?"

"Yes, she's going to stay in the house with the kids."

"All right, then, after announcing the divorce I'd say something like this: 'Kids, there are a couple of things your mother and I want you to know. One is about why we're getting a divorce. Sometimes children blame themselves for breakups. But this divorce is about us, not about you two. Mom and I have some problems we can't solve but we both love you guys very much and nothing that's happened between us will or could ever change that.

" 'We also know you're both wondering about the changes that lie ahead. Inevitably there'll be some. But your mother and I have agreed that you're going to stay here in the house with her. So some of the big things— your home, neighborhood friends, and school—still will be the same. That's also true for your relationship with me. You'll still be seeing lots of your dad.'

"At this point, George, stop and give Billy and Megan a chance to react. If Billy says, 'I'm really mad at you guys,' reflect that feeling in a statement like 'You're angry about the divorce,' but then step aside. Do the same if Megan says, 'I feel terrible, Daddy'—reflect, but don't reply.

"Some hard things are probably going to be said tomorrow night and on other nights in the months to come, George. But if you allow yourself to get defensive on these occasions, Megan and Billy won't have a chance to ventilate their anger and pain, which means these feelings will go underground and pop up a year from now in social, personal, and academic problems. For the next few months, let them have the floor.

"Another thing I'd also avoid tomorrow night is a detailed discussion of why you and Elizabeth are separating. Your news will be overwhelming enough; the kids won't have any energy left to process the whys and wherefores of the breakup. And there's always the chance that this kind of discussion can lead to more fighting between you and Elizabeth, which is the last thing Megan and Billy will need to see tomorrow night. If you're asked about reasons for the divorce, stick to generalities like 'Mom and Dad just find that we can't live with one another anymore' or 'We have some problems we can't solve.'

"One common fear you probably won't hear voiced right away is 'Dad, will the divorce make us poorer?' Billy and Megan will be too busy processing your news to begin thinking about its financial implications. Sometime in the next week or two, though, it will dawn on them that a general belt-tightening may be required. And that's when you start hearing questions like 'Dad, will we still be able to afford my horseback-riding lessons?' and 'Dad, what about the hockey clinic I signed up for?' "

One former program dad, Carl Rubenstein, made the mistake a lot of men make after a breakup—in his anxiety about finances he overlooked the special meaning ongoing activities like ballet can assume in the eyes of a child of a divorce. When the rest of your world turns upside down, a regularly scheduled activity can become a powerful symbol of order and stability, and if it's eliminated without warning it can turn a normal post-divorce tailspin into a nose dive.

Carl, who was planning just such an abrupt end to his daughter's ballet classes, laughed when I told him this. "Jenny's going to thank me, Ron," he insisted. "She doesn't even like the classes." But when Jenny was informed the next day that for financial reasons Friday would be her last day of ballet, instead of thanking Carl, she jumped out of his car yelling, "I hate you, Daddy. I hate you!"

If activities have to be cut, they have to be cut. But give children three or four weeks to absorb the news and be ready with a list of alternatives. YMCAs, CYOs, Boy Scouts, and Girl Scouts offer lots of low-cost activities that can be just as much fun for a kid as twenty-dollar-an-hour riding lessons or one-hundred-dollar hockey clinics.

The second area in which divorcing parents need to cooperate involves their relationship with the kids. Study after study has shown that another key factor in a child's post-divorce recovery is *ongoing and regular paternal contact.* This is most immediately apparent for boys, who often respond to a paternal loss by developing personal social and academic problems. Girls do better in the short run, but recent studies indicate there may be a "sleeper effect" of broken paternal contact which shows up in the form of relationship problems.

Initially, most divorced dads don't think this is going to be a problem. But a dozen ugly scenes at the doorstep during pickups and a half dozen suddenly canceled weekends and you may find yourself feeling like Harry Wilson, another former program dad.

When I ran into Harry at Faneuil Hall a couple of months ago, he told me he hadn't seen his kids in nearly a year. And when I asked him why, he said, "Ron, I just got tired of all the petty humiliations. Whenever I'd come by to pick up Jim and Reg, my ex-wife would make me wait outside on the lawn, and when she finally did decide to send them out, it was usually on the arm of her smirking boyfriend and in clothes that belonged in a Goodwill shop. Who needs that!"

Harry was wrong, of course. *Nothing* should be allowed to stand between a man and his children. But the fact is that an angry or vindictive wife can wear away at your resolve. Harry, for example, said he finally gave up on regular visits when he arrived at his former house one Friday afternoon expecting to pick up his kids and instead found a note pinned to the door which said:

> Sorry for the last minute change of plans. But mother's sick and needs my help. Am taking the kids with me.
>
> Cheers,
> Betty

Regular, sustained contact with children is impossible unless a man remains on reasonably civilized terms with his ex-wife. And there are several things you'll need to do

in order to maintain a good relationship. One is to antic-
ipate future conflicts and take steps beforehand to prevent
them.

The first place I'd look for potential conflicts to arise
is with custody and visitation. In most divorce and sepa-
ration agreements, a father's access to his children is defined by the phrase "reasonable visitation." I don't know
who invented the term, but I do know that for two people
who may have trouble agreeing that they need a divorce,
it's a sure-fire recipe for trouble.

If George and Elizabeth follow the typical pattern,
she'll interpret "reasonable visitation" to mean every other
weekend except when she wants to bring the kids to her
parents' or when Megan has a Saturday-morning gym class.
George will interpret it to mean every weekend except
when he has a date or is away on business, plus a couple
of major holidays a year. And the two of them will end
up doing more fighting than they do now, which won't do
much for Megan and Billy or for George's relationship
with Elizabeth.

There are three ways to deal with this problem. One
is to ask for joint physical custody of the children. You'll
automatically avoid visitation fights with this arrangement
because it divides all parental rights and responsibilities
evenly. You'd each get the kids a designated number of
days and nights per week and you'd both retain an equal
voice in decisions affecting their well-being. In order to
make joint physical custody work, though, you'd also have
to live near one another; otherwise the commute between
your house and your wife's would be too much for the
kids.

The other option is to cede your wife sole custody,
which is the arrangement nine out of ten divorcing parents

opt for. And while it can produce frictions, it won't if you make sure your visitation rights are clearly spelled out in the agreement. It should specify the time and frequency of your visits, the number of days you get the children for vacations and which month, and also what, if any, holidays you get to spend with them. This way, there won't be any nasty fights later over who gets the kids for Thanksgiving.

The third choice, one which is much less frequent, is to ask for sole custody. However, to make this choice work it's essential to have the support of one's former spouse.

"Have you thought about what kind of visitation rights you'd want?" I asked George.

"Every weekend plus Christmas, Thanksgiving, Labor Day, and two weeks in the summer for vacation. But what Elizabeth's probably willing to give me is one week of vacation, plus every other weekend, except—"

"I know, except when Megan has a Saturday-morning gym class or Elizabeth wants to pack the kids off to her mother's. That leaves your respective positions on visitation pretty far apart and you in a dilemma, George. How do you push for more time with Megan and Billy, and yet not so alienate Elizabeth in the process that she starts putting herself between you and them?

"I don't have a magical solution. But I think you'll find Elizabeth a lot more receptive if you use your Self-expression skills when the two of you sit down to talk about visitation. That means stating your point of view honestly but without finger pointing or accusation.

"Let's suppose, during your talk, Elizabeth says to you, 'George, I've thought it over, every other weekend is enough.' How would you use Self-expression to reply to her?"

"My relationship with the kids means a lot to me,

Elizabeth, and I'm not going to be able to sustain it if I only see them twice a month."

"Good. You've made your feelings clear, but without blaming Elizabeth, which will keep her in a receptive frame of mind. You'll find her even more receptive, though, if you reflect her point of view in your statement. You said she gave up a career to stay home with Megan and Billy. That was a big sacrifice and you should acknowledge it by saying something like 'Elizabeth, I realize how much you've given up for the kids, and I appreciate that. But I've got my own relationship with them; and I won't be able to sustain it if I only see them every other week.'

"This declaration won't make Elizabeth your number-one fan again, but it might make her think, 'George isn't such a bad guy after all.' And with that semihappy thought in mind, she'll be much more likely to say yes when you then say, 'Look, Elizabeth, instead of fighting about visitation, why don't we sit down and try to resolve our differences through negotiation?' which is the other program skill that has relevance for your situation.

"The two of you already know what your problem is, so you can skip the technique's first step and go right to its heart—drawing up a list of solutions that reflect your respective points of view. Yours is that frequency is essential to a close relationship with Megan and Billy. What visitation rights would satisfy that position?"

"Every weekend, plus Christmas, Thanksgiving, Labor Day and two weeks' vacation time."

"Do you have a fallback position?"

"Every weekend plus Christmas or Thanksgiving and one week's vacation. My bottom line would be no weeks' vacation, but everything else."

"All right, George, any solution Elizabeth agrees to will have to reflect her career sacrifices. And you've done that by giving her sole custody. Is there anything else that might affect her negotiating position?"

"Brigid Kearney."

"Elizabeth's mother?"

"Yes, she and Elizabeth are very close; Liz is always taking the kids to her mother's house."

"Okay, what if Elizabeth said, 'George, give me ten weekends a year for visits to my mother's and every other weekend is yours'?"

"I'd say, 'Elizabeth, what will you give me in return?' "

"Suppose she said, 'In return, George, you can have a week of vacation time.' "

"But no Christmas or Thanksgiving?"

"George, Elizabeth's got her own interests now; and she's going to look after them. She's not a part of you anymore."

George took a cigarette from the pack of Benson & Hedges on the table and lit it. "I've smoked a half pack of these this morning.

"I know Elizabeth's her own person now, Ron. I realized that yesterday morning. I was walking to my cab when I turned around halfway down the driveway and saw Elizabeth standing on the back porch with a plastic garbage can in her hands. I've seen her standing on that back porch every day since we bought the house, but yesterday she looked different. She had on the same blue turtleneck and the same preoccupied expression she always wears when she's doing chores, but yesterday morning it all came together differently.

"Funny isn't it, you can know someone, in every way

you can know another human being, then, one morning you turn around in your driveway and she's gone and there's a stranger standing there."

"It is strange, George."

"I have another picture of Elizabeth, Ron. It's of her coming down her dormitory stairs behind a girl named Bobbi, the night we met. Elizabeth was wearing a green plaid jumper and the same preoccupied expression she had yesterday, which makes her look prim. Bobbi looked like her name and I remember getting mad at Bill Carlson, the guy who'd arranged the dates for the two of us, for giving himself Annette Funicello and me June Allyson. But as soon as Elizabeth smiled at me, I stopped being mad.

"That picture's all in gold, Ron. The September night, the way the light in the dormitory hall lit the trees outside, the hopeful expression on the faces of the boys under the trees waiting for their blind dates, being twenty and having your whole life laid out in front of you like a magic carpet, and Elizabeth walking down the stairs behind Bobbi in her green plaid jumper looking prim and preoccupied. Now, I have the matching bookend; a stranger in a blue turtle-neck standing on my back porch, sixteen years later, on a cold March morning with a plastic garbage can in her hand.

"It's like there's music, then there's no music, and once it stops, everything looks different."

"I guess the next few months are going to be filled with yesterday mornings."

"There'll be some bad moments, George. It'll hurt the first time you walk into your living room and see your favorite chair missing or you hear Billy or Megan say, 'Dad, Mom's having the septic tank cleaned early this year.' But that's part of the natural order of things in a divorce. And it's not just that Elizabeth's suddenly become a different person, George. With the breakup the center of gravity shifts in the Phelan family. Elizabeth becomes the head of the house, and another thing you're going to have to do, if you want to maintain a civilized relationship with her—and through her a close one with Megan and Billy—is to accept this shift with reasonable grace. Did you see *Shoot the Moon?*"

"Albert Finney and Diane Keaton? No, I missed it."

"Pick it up when you get a VCR for your new apartment. It's a good cautionary tale; it shows what happens when a man fights this transfer of power. It's also very good at dramatizing how little details like a new chair or an absent picture can work on the terrible sense of powerlessness men feel after a divorce."

In that film, things like a new shade of eye liner on his wife or the mention of a new friend by one of his daughters has an almost physical impact on the Albert Finney character. He reels from one change to another, until finally, at the end of the movie, he's so frustrated and hurt he erupts and drives his car through his wife's new tennis court.

The moral of this story isn't that a divorced man should be a reed to his former wife's every little breeze, but simply that, for everyone's sake, including his own, he should accept the inevitable and acknowledge that divorce changes a man's status in the family.

In terms of George's status in the Phelan family this means fighting hard for his bottom-line position on visitation—every weekend with the kids. But it also means realizing that Elizabeth's new position and persona give her the power and will to demand concessions like holidays and ten weekends a year for visits to her mother. And beyond visitation, it means realizing that while Megan and

Billy will always be a part of his life, Elizabeth, their living-room furniture, and a lot of other things are now going to become part of someone else's.

Elizabeth will appreciate his grace and good sense and George will see her appreciation reflected in the way she upholds and supports his position with Billy and Megan.

Paying support payments regularly will also help maintain the status quo. There will be times when this will be inconvenient, and other times when it will be just plain hard. But if he expects Elizabeth to support his wishes, he has to show her he expects to support his children.

Remember that withholding support payments for any reason is, first of all, illegal—and second, it's self-defeating. George could hurt Elizabeth, but he'd hurt Billy and Megan to hurt her, and I know he wouldn't want to do that.

His protection in the case of visitation violations is their tightly worded agreement. If Elizabeth tries to break it, he can remind her of its provisions, and if she goes ahead and breaks it anyway, he can call his lawyer. But he can't use money to punish her because he'll only end up punishing his children.

Bobby Giannano, a father in the program the year before, learned this lesson the hard way. Last year, one of his support checks bounced and a few days later when he arrived at his ex-wife Carol's to pick up Carla, his five-year-old, Bobby found her standing on the front porch in a pair of overalls that had his bounced check and a note pinned to the bib. The note said, "Dear Dad: If you don't give Mommy money, I won't have any food to eat."

Bobby is not one to turn the other cheek. So Sunday night when Carol opened the front door, she found Carla standing on the front porch in the same pair of overalls with another note pinned to her bib. This one said, "Dear

Mommy, who is that man you've been having over to the house for sleep-over dates?"

I told Bobby that he and Carol ought to be ashamed of themselves for turning Carla into their Avenging Angel. Putting a child into the middle of parental fights is like picking at a wound. Every fight reopens it and, if the fights go on and on and the child is always in the middle of them, instead of healing cleanly the wound festers and sores begin to develop an ugly layer of scar tissue in the form of emotional and school problems.

Fighting's inevitable in a divorce. Just be sure not to do it in front of the children. *Involvement in parental conflict* is the third factor that can affect a child's post-divorce recovery. Agree to keep fights to yourselves. And that's easy to do if the two of you follow four basic ground rules.

The first is, don't criticize each other in front of the kids. Children, and most especially children of divorce, want and need to believe in their parents; it gives their lives a center. And it's very hard for a center to hold if all the youngsters hear are remarks like "Your mother let you out of the house in that wrinkled dress?" or "Kids, your father won't be over tonight, he's got a date. That's how much he cares about you."

The second ground rule is, don't undermine each other's authority. You may not like all of your wife's rules, but if she doesn't want your children to have ice cream or Coke or Hostess Twinkies, don't let them cheat with you. She'll be grateful for your cooperation and she'll return the favor by respecting and upholding your authority with them.

The third ground rule is, never use a child as a messenger the way Bobby and Carol Giannano did. If relations between you and your wife sour to the point where you're not speaking, use a neutral intermediary like a mutual friend to relay essential information, or put the information in a letter. But if you do that, send the letter. Giving it to a child to hand-deliver means your ex-wife probably will open it in his presence, and if she doesn't like what's inside, she's likely to criticize you in front of him.

I told George, the last ground rule is, never let fights interfere with your visits. Being able to count on seeing you will be too important to the kids. Your ex-wife should understand that and you should, too.

"Seeing my kids is going to be important to me, too, Ron."

"I know you feel that way now, George. But what about a year from now when life, in the form of a new girlfriend or a new circle of acquaintances, intervenes? Are you still going to feel the same? Beyond Elizabeth, your own relationship with the kids will be essential to their recovery. And if they know you've begun skipping your weekends with them to spend your Saturdays and Sundays on Cape Cod or in New York with your new amour or new friends, it's going to hurt—a lot.

"In the long run, Megan and Billy will benefit more from an every-other-weekend schedule that's strictly observed than from an every-weekend schedule that sometimes is and sometimes isn't. Remember that, George.

"Also, remember that when the three of you are together you should act like a dad, not a social director. After a divorce, a lot of men fall into the trap of thinking, 'My kids won't like me if I don't entertain them.' So a weekend at Dad's becomes like a Caribbean cruise for senior citizens. Everyone's up at eight for breakfast at McDonald's, then it's off to a crafts show, then a movie, and then a museum, which keeps everyone busy, but doesn't leave the kids and Dad time for what everyone needs most, a quiet talk together.

"In the years to come, if Billy and Megan are going to look back on their weekends with you as a light in the window in an otherwise dark time, it's going to be because of the talks you shared, not the museums or crafts shows you visited. I know encouraging open, unselfconscious talk won't be easy. Divorce destroys the dailiness that greases it. But there are a couple of things you can do to restore the honest, intimate conversation it fosters. One is to assign Billy and Megan some regular weekend chores. A lot of men are afraid to do this because they think their children will be reluctant to visit Dad if visiting him means having to help with the dishes or the vacuuming. But chores like these make a boy or girl feel like a part of Dad's life again and they're also a good, natural springboard for conversation.

"Activities like checkers or hiking or fishing also can restore a measure of dailiness to a divorced father and his child and they, too, leave the door open to the kind of good honest talk that leaves everyone feeling better.

"The listening skills you learned in the project are another way of maintaining an element of intimacy in an every-weekend or every-other-weekend relationship. This is especially true for reflection. Billy and Megan will be full of hidden messages during the next year, and knowing how to help them identify and talk about those messages not only reduces the risk of their acting them out, it also gives you a chance to display paternal understanding at a moment in their lives when they'll both be craving it.

"Do you remember how hidden messages signal themselves?"

"Non sequiturs, dissonance, out-of-character behavior . . ."

"That's the sign you'll probably see the most of,
George."

"Out-of-character behavior?"

"Yes, it's very common after a divorce and usually it's
an indication that the breakup is really gnawing at the child.
A story another program dad, Caine Deutch, told me is a
case in point."

About four months after Caine and his wife separated,
Caine noticed that his normally easygoing, sociable eleven-
year-old, Diane, was suddenly criticizing all her friends.
Diane hated Friend A for doing this, Friend B for doing
that, and Friend C for doing something else.

Caine was pretty sure that what Diane really hated
was the divorce. But he knew that if he approached the
subject head-on, Diane would jump. So he waited and
picked his moment carefully, which happened to be a
lovely May afternoon. He and Diane had been together
all day, and now relaxed and cozy, they were sitting under
a weeping willow in the Public Garden sharing a bag of
roasted peanuts and watching the swan boats glide by.

Caine opened the conversation by picking up on a
remark that Diane had made at breakfast. "I was surprised
this morning when you told me you and Debbie were on
the outs," he said. "I thought Deb was your best friend,
Diane."

Diane allowed that while this may have been true
once, it no longer was. "Debbie's gotten real stuck-up,"
she said.

"She acts like she thinks she's better than you?" Caine
asked.

"Uh-huh, all the kids do, Dad."

Caine knew enough about Diane and about kids and divorce to know that her remark was very likely a reflection of the shame and inferiority many children feel after a marital breakup. But he also knew that Diane would jump if he came out and said, "Hon, are you afraid your friends think they're better than you because their parents are still together and yours aren't?" So he offered another reflection: "You think all the kids look down on you, hon?"

"And that pushed the button, George. All Diane's pain and shame about the divorce came tumbling out in a headlong rush."

"What did Caine do then, Ron?"

"Nothing, he just let Diane talk. I'd suggest you do the same with Megan and Billy, not only tomorrow night, but for the next four or five months. The more they talk about their pain and anguish now, the less likely it is that you'll find yourselves dealing with the consequences of these unvoiced feelings a year from now.

"And if it's Billy who starts doing most of the acting out, it could pose a serious discipline problem for Elizabeth."

"She handles him pretty well."

"She handles him pretty well now, George. But what about two years from now, when you're not there every day and Billy's grown half a head taller and thirty pounds heavier than Elizabeth? Is he going to pick up his room when she tells him to or is he going to look at the physical differences between them and say, 'No, Mom, you can't push me around; I'll pick up my room when I'm ready'?

"The data on boys and divorce suggest he's going to say no and they also suggest that if Billy does mount a challenge to Elizabeth's authority, she'll respond by belittling and undermining him. This kind of vicious circle is very common among sons and their single mothers and it's a chief reason why boys tend to be immediately more vulnerable to the effects of a divorce. So one other thing you can do to ease your kids' post-divorce adjustment, and, in particular, Billy's, is to make it clear to all concerned that while your address may change, your rules of discipline and readiness to enforce them haven't.

"Elizabeth will be grateful to you for your help in this area, and Billy, though he won't tell you until he's thirty, even more so. Love speaks to a child in many voices, George, and one of the most nourishing of them is the voice that says, 'Dad cares enough about you to show you right from wrong.'

"You know who we haven't talked about yet—you. In its own way the next year is going to be as hard for you as it'll be for Megan and Billy. You'll find yourself full of strange thoughts and feelings and alarming mood swings. The best place to deal with these reactions is a support group."

Some divorced dads use their friends to help them through this transitional period; others join one of the formal support groups that have sprung up over the last few years like the discussion group we have for single dads at the Fatherhood Project. At a time like this, talk is just as therapeutic to an adult as it is to a child.

10
Surviving Stepfathering

On a warm April morning, when the sky above my window was as bright and cloudless as the promise of spring itself and the Charles River below it was as clear and smooth as a sheet of blue-tinted Plexiglas, Roger Levine arrived in my office bearing a deep Caribbean tan, a bottle of 100-proof rum, and a big problem. The tan was acquired on Martinique during a two-week honeymoon with his new wife, Ann; the rum was a thank-you present for a wedding gift I'd sent the Levines; and the big problem, well, I'm sure each and every one of America's thirteen million stepfathers would find it familiar. Because, on occasion, each and every one of them has faced the dilemma Roger had faced a few nights earlier when, just as he was about to settle in with the "CBS Evening News," his new stepson, Noah, pointed an aggrieved finger at the TV set and said, "Hey, Roger, I want to watch 'Wheel of Fortune,' turn the station."

"I hate 'Wheel of Fortune' and everything it represents," Roger said. "But Noah's Ann's son; also, it's her TV and I'm living in her house."

"So," I said, "you wondered, 'What do I do now?' "

"I tried being reasonable, Ron. I told him, 'Noah, the TV programs you watch say a lot about you. And what "Wheel of Fortune" says, I don't think a smart boy like you would want said about Noah!'

"But then Ann accused me of being pretentious. Or to be more precise, she said, 'Roger, you're being an old fart.' I was furious, but—"

"You wondered, 'What do I do now?' I'll bet you find yourself wondering that a lot these days, Rog."

"Twice this morning alone. The first time when Ann's fourteen-year-old, Donovan, asked me to walk the dog, which happens to be her chore, not mine, and the second time a few minutes later, when the phone rang. I picked it up, and guess who was on the other end of the line?"

"Your wife's ex-husband."

Roger nodded. "Also my son called. Max expects us to spend the weekend with him, but Ann wants me to spend it on Martha's Vineyard with her and her kids. These days, I feel like I'm living inside an anxiety attack."

"If it's any consolation, Roger, most new stepfathers do. Have you and Ann talked about any of these issues?"

Roger smiled ruefully. "We thought love would see us through."

"It'll help, Rog. But it's not going to tell you what to say the next time Noah wants to watch 'Wheel of Fortune,' or Donovan asks you to walk the dog, or you find yourself on the phone with their father. And I'm afraid I can't tell you what to say, either."

"Who can, Ron?"

"You and Ann and Max and Noah and Donovan and

time, Roger—above all, time. I know you think you already know a great deal about fathering. But you'll find that your experience with Max isn't a very good guide to what lies ahead with Noah and Donovan.

"For one thing, you don't have the free hand shaping your relationship with them that you did with Max. You'll have Ann's thoughts and feelings to contend with, and their father's, and Max's.

"For another, the issues you face as a stepdad are different. With Max, who came to you with a clean slate, the chief issue was 'How do I facilitate this child's development?' With Noah and Donovan, who come to you with a set of biological parents, unique histories, and already formed personalities, the chief issues are 'How do I fit into their lives?' and 'How do they fit into mine?'

"You'll also find that the lack of a biological tie makes a subtle, or maybe not so subtle, difference in everyone's attitude. There won't be the sense of unconditional acceptance you and Max and every other biologically linked father and child share. You and your stepkids will love each other because of the things you do for one another, not in spite of them.

"In many ways, Roger, the difference between your first experience of fathering and this one will be the difference between starting your own firm and joining someone else's. With Max you started your own, and that gave you a free hand to create your rules and guidelines. With Noah and Donovan you're joining an ongoing concern, with its own established rules, culture, relationships, and ways of doing things."

We have a program for stepdads here at the Fatherhood Project, and some of the men are as close to their stepchildren as biological fathers; others are more like big brothers or uncles. But whatever their particular experience, I think all of them would say the same thing: if you want to make a successful place for yourself in your new firm, you'll have to do two things.

The first is to be patient. Establishing moral authority over a child and building a bond of love and trust with him takes two or three years, and if you're not prepared to spend that time, you could find yourself becoming very disappointed very fast.

The other thing you must do is stay flexible. Ultimately, the kind of stepdad you become is going to be determined jointly by *all* the members of your firm, and if you aren't flexible enough to accept the possibility that they may see your role a little differently than you do, you could find the firm a very difficult place to work.

Not only will all these people have an important say in how close you get to your stepkids, but also how great a financial contribution you make to them, how much authority and discipline you exercise over them, and how much time you spend together. Henceforth, they also will have a say in what kind of father you are to your own child.

And the most important member of your new firm will be your new wife. More than anyone else, she'll determine the size and importance of your stepparenting role, and in a more subtle way, she'll also have a very important say in your relationship with your child.

Ideally, the time for a discussion of responsibilities, chores, and authority in your new family is before the wedding. You should know exactly how large a financial contribution you'll have to make to your stepfamily, the nature of your responsibilities to it, what the visiting arrangements will be for your child, what your stepchildren will call you, how you and your wife will resolve clashes over values, and how much of her parental authority she'll share with you.

"Can I give you some advice, Roger? Initially—and by initially, I mean for the first year or so—don't overreact if you find Ann backsliding on her part of the authority-sharing agreement. She and Noah and Donovan have been together as a single family for how long now?"

"Five years."

"Often, a woman who's headed a household for that long develops such a deep and intimate bond with her kids that she finds it very hard to let anyone else exercise authority over them. No matter what she says or thinks, she can't quite bring herself to let go."

One of our program stepdads, Sam Freebarin, complained to me bitterly about this problem. At the time, Sam's stepson, Phil, was six and had, like most six-year-olds, developed a distressing fondness for revolting language. Every other word out of his mouth was "poopy brain" and "diarrhea head."

Sam couldn't stand it, and, ostensibly, neither could his wife and Phil's mother, Carol Ann. Every time Sam said, "Carol Ann, we should correct Phil when he talks like that," Carol Ann would say, "You're right, Sam, we should." But nearly every time Sam tried, Carol Ann would jump in and say, "Stop, Sam, Phil's only six. Don't bully him like that."

Before the marriage, Carol Ann had agreed to give Sam an equal voice in matters of authority, limit setting, and child rearing. But like many stepdads before him, Sam was discovering that what you're told isn't necessarily what you get, in this department.

When he asked me what to do, I told him the first thing he'd have to do to make his situation more tolerable was learn to be patient. A woman who's had sole responsibility for her kids needs a little time to adjust to the idea of sharing it with another adult, and Carol Ann hadn't had much time. The language problem developed a few months after the wedding.

My second piece of advice to Sam was "Use your Self-awareness skill." I knew the undercutting was making him furious, but I also knew that Sam didn't know that. And remember: anger that remains unidentified often goes underground, transforms itself, and reappears in the form of the Rubber Band's explosive fury or the Tin Man's mechanical cool.

Fortunately, Sam was able to avoid both. Once he put a name on his anger, he was able to start managing it in the sense that he was able to tell himself: "All right, I'm mad at being undercut. But I have to put my reaction into perspective. Phil's been Carol Ann's sole responsibility for three years; it's only natural that she'd need time to adjust to me as a co-parent." So he never turned into a Mike Danzig or a Harold Reddiger.

"Use your Self-expression skills" was my last piece of advice to Sam. Saying, "Hey, stop contradicting me; you agreed to give me equal authority over Phil," would have gotten Carol Ann's back up. Carol Ann would have felt Sam was overstepping himself. And, at a minimum, that could have threatened their parental agreement and maybe even hurt their marriage.

The form of Self-expression Sam used, however, allowed him to avoid these hazards. Every time Carol Ann undercut him, he would say, "Hon, I understand how close you and Phil are, and I know how hard that makes it for you to see me correct him, but for everyone's sake, we have to make our agreement work." This statement allowed Sam to make his point, but without finger pointing or accusation, and, in the process, to tip his hat to Carol Ann's maternal concerns.

By the end of the first year, after several similar discussions, Carol Ann had pretty much come around. If Sam criticized Phil, she didn't intervene, and what was probably even more important, if Phil was disrespectful or rude, she'd tell him, "Please don't talk to your stepfather that way; he respects you, respect him."

I should point out that not every woman will go as far as Carol Ann. Many mothers insist on remaining the primary voice of authority in the house—either because they feel that it is their due as the child's biological parent or because they dislike the masculine limit-setting style, which even at its most relaxed tends to be more directive than the female style.

Should your new wife turn out to be such a mother, I'd suggest you submit to her wishes—as a stepparent you really don't have any other choice—and aim for an agreement that, at least, gives you some power. At the very least, try to get her to support your authority on certain issues. It's very, very hard for a stepfather to deal with a statement like "You're not my father, you can't tell me what to do" without the support of the child's biological parent. And as a bottom line, you should insist on having some input, even if it's only indirect, on disciplinary matters. And by indirect, I mean that she be willing to give you a fair and open hearing if you have a problem with some aspect of her children's behavior.

If she says no even to this, you have two alternatives. One is to find a psychologist or agency that specializes in stepfamily counseling. The other is to pray and play for time. Ultimately, a stepfather is obeyed, not because Mom says he should be, but because he is loved and respected. But it takes several years for those feelings to take root and grow, and if you don't have the support of the child's mother in the meantime, it could be an awfully long year or two.

I told Roger that Noah and Donovan also are important members of his new firm. "If Ann is the key, they're the door. Whatever she may want for you as a stepdad, unless they want it too, you're probably going to experience stepfathering as a spectator sport. How old are they now?"

"Six and fourteen."

"Initially, you'll find that their age and sex will have an important influence on their willingness to accept and start building a relationship with you. I don't want to make either variable sound hard and fast. Over time, love is more powerful than both. But the research does show that, at the outset, being a boy or girl, or younger or older, does affect a stepchild's degree of receptivity.

"Roughly speaking, boys are more receptive than girls and younger children more receptive than older ones and adolescents."

"I can expect an easier time with Noah, then, Ron?"

"Roughly speaking, yes. A six-year-old's personality and loyalties haven't been firmly shaped yet, and that will leave the door open a little wider for you. And so, in a way, will Noah's helplessness. When you and he go out together, he's going to need your hand to cross the street, and your voice to order him an ice cream, and your strength to lift him up on his bike, and your height to reach up and get him the Froot Loops. And seeing you fill all these needs is going to make him think, 'Gee, Roger takes care of me,' and it's only a short walk from that thought to 'Gee, I like being with Roger.'

"The sex similarity also will help. You're a male, you have a son not much older than Noah. So he'll find that you're surprisingly good at understanding his thoughts and feelings. In time, he may even discover that you're better at understanding them than his mother. And if he does, you'll discover that when Noah has a problem or wants some advice, you may be the person in the family he turns to.

"With Donovan, these variables will work against, rather than for, you. She's old enough to remember that it was her dad who reached up and got the Froot Loops, who lifted her up on her bike, and who took her hand at the curb. And the glow of these memories will probably put an edge on Donovan's attitude. She'll be more stand-offish and wary.

"The gender difference can further complicate your relationship with her, Roger. Being male you're going to find her thoughts and feelings harder to understand, and being female, she's going to find yours equally impenetrable. So when Donovan has a problem or wants some advice, she'll probably continue doing what she's been doing all along—turning to Ann for help. And that will make it harder for you and her to build the kind of intimacies that deepen the father-child relationship.

"Just remember, though, Roger, these factors are not immutable. Age and sex may have shaped the attitude of the Donovan—and the Noah—who welcomed you home after Martinique, but you'll be the one who shapes the attitudes of the two kids who welcome you home a year from now. Ultimately, how wide each opens the door to you will depend on what you say and don't say, and what you do and don't do. And if you want to find their doors wide open a year from today, one thing you should do now is stand back a little.

"I know that sounds paradoxical. But if you stand back in the beginning and give a stepchild the time and emotional room he needs to adjust to your presence, more often than not, later you'll find he shows his appreciation by walking over from his side of the court and extending a hand across the net.

"Roger, you look puzzled."

"I am, Ron. Does that mean if I'm taking Max to Fenway to see a Red Sox–Yankee game, I shouldn't ask Noah if he'd like to come along?"

"No, no, by all means ask Noah. While it's important not to push or insist, it's also important to let a stepchild know 'I'm ready to build a relationship when you are.' You can do this directly by telling him, or, better still, you can use your listening skills to signal your readiness the way Sam Freebarin did when his stepson, Phil, fell in love with Robin Hood."

You know six-year-olds; when something strikes their fancy, they often become obsessed by it, and that's how Phil became about the old Errol Flynn movie *The Adventures of Robin Hood*. Night after night, Phil would sit in the den watching a video of it.

Sam knew enough about kids to know that the road to their hearts usually lies through their interests, and he also knew enough about the way they communicate to know that a pattern or repetition is a signal of a key interest. And as he listened to Phil talk about Robin Hood, he noticed a pattern. Whatever other aspects of the movie he mentioned, Phil always came back to the characters' tunics and weapons. When you address a child's key interest, it usually makes a child open up, and that's what it did to Phil. For the first six months of their relationship, he hadn't said much beyond uh-huh to his stepfather, but the day Sam observed that the Sheriff of Nottingham's tunics were longer and his sword bigger than Robin Hood's, Phil couldn't restrain himself. Here were issues he had been pondering deeply for weeks and now that someone had finally shown a flicker of interest in his interest, out came tumbling all his insights. For the next half hour, Sam was given a detailed description of the number, size, and potential deadliness of the Sheriff's and Robin Hood's weapons and the cut, color, size, and general snappiness of their tunics. Knowing Sam was interested in his interest, Phil had opened the door a little. The next night, before putting *Robin Hood* in the VCR, he asked Sam if he'd like to join him. Seven nights and five viewings later, the door opened even wider.

It isn't often that a man's able to put a finger on the turning point in his relationship with a child, but Sam has no doubt that the turning point in his relationship with Phil came on that seventh night when, midway through his fifth viewing of the movie, he turned to his stepson and said: "You know, I hate to say this, Phil."

"Say what?" Phil asked.

"Well," Sam replied, "the Sheriff of Nottingham may be a bad guy, but he's a way better dresser than Robin Hood."

In all the time they'd been together, Sam had made many jokes, big and small, but this was the first time he could remember his stepson had ever allowed himself to smile at one.

When Noah becomes obsessed by Dwight Evans's batting average or Donovan isn't asked to the dance by the boy of her dreams, Roger can also use the listening skills to tell them, "I'm ready." Having a sympathetic adult there who's eager to listen not only to their words but also to the feelings and thoughts beneath those words will make both kids think, "Gee, Roger really does want to get close to me."

"Assuming their father doesn't interfere, Ron."

"Are you worried that he might?"

"I don't know what to expect from him."

"Well, one thing you can definitely expect, Roger, is that he'll also have an important voice in deciding what kind of stepfather you become. And that's true even if he's more or less disappeared from the scene. You'll feel his presence in Noah's and Donovan's attitudes, values, and memories, and you'll also feel it in your pocketbook, since whatever financial support he doesn't provide, you'll have to. What's his status?"

"Oh, Robert Burke is still very much with us. Noah and Donovan see him every weekend, and he also takes them for a part of each summer. I'll say this for him, he's a pretty conscientious father."

"Can I give you another piece of advice then, Roger? Key your role to his. Stepfathering doesn't have many rules, but one of them is the inverse-proportion rule. The larger the biological father's role in a child's emotional life, usually the smaller the stepfather's."

This rule has several implications. One is that a child has room in his heart for only one active, involved father, and if his biological father is already occupying that room, his stepdad shouldn't try to force his way in and stage a coup d'état. In time, I'm sure both Noah and Donovan will come to love and respect Roger, but if they're already close to their father, Roger should accept the fact that they're not going to love and respect him the way they do Robert.

Dads who remain close to their children after a divorce also tend to be memorialized in word and deed. So another implication of the inverse-proportion rule is that you'll have to learn to live with their dad as an invisible presence in your home. You'll see his smile in his children and hear his voice in theirs. You'll probably even have to learn to live with his physical presence in the form of photos and mementos of him the kids keep in their rooms.

You may not like looking at these, but don't take them personally. They're not aimed at you or your self-esteem. A divorce is an enormous trauma for a youngster, and building a kind of shrine to the absent but loved parent is one of the ways kids deal with this trauma.

Involved dads also tend to retain an important voice in limit-setting and disciplining policies. So the inverse-proportion rule also means respecting his authority in these areas. You may not like all his policies; you may think that nine o'clock and not the ten o'clock curfew he's set is more appropriate for a teenager. But when you find yourself disagreeing with his rules, you might remind yourself of something one of our stepdads at the project told me.

"Philosophically, the kids' father and I couldn't be further apart," this stepdad said. "But I know he cares about the kids and keeps a close eye on them. So when he sets a policy about curfews or study times, I respect it."

"Have you met Robert yet, Roger?"

"Once."

"Well, let me pass on some rules that will make your relationship with him easier—on you, on him, on Ann, and on Noah and Donovan. The first rule is, whatever your true feelings about him, don't criticize him in front of the kids. If he turns out to be one of those men who's always a month or two late with his support check or an hour or two late for pickups, this won't be an easy rule to follow. But Robert is Noah and Donovan's dad and hearing his replacement denigrate him will not only hurt them, it could irreparably damage your relationship with them. Disputes about pickup times, finances, and other matters should be conducted out of the kids' sight and hearing.

"The second rule is, let Ann and Robert handle their disputes. By all means give Ann your support, but try not to become a physical presence in their arguments. The sight of you sitting next to Ann on the other side of the kitchen table or the sound of your voice in the background during a phone conversation could raise Robert's back so high he becomes insensible to reason.

"Unfortunately, there's also a third rule, Rog. Sometimes an ex-husband's behavior becomes so disruptive or the communications between him and his former wife sour so much that a stepfather has no choice but to intervene. Should you find yourself in this unhappy position, remember, in discussions with Robert always stick to the facts and only the facts. Explain to him why his behavior has become a problem for Ann or you or your family and suggest some possible solutions. But don't allow your feelings or Robert's to draw the two of you into a discussion of personal matters. You could very well end up at one another's throats and that won't help anyone. If Robert remains insensitive to your pleas, have Ann call her lawyer.

"Max will also influence your stepfathering through the guilt rule; it goes something like this: 'The less time, affection, and love a man feels able to give his own child, the more reluctant he becomes to give them to anyone else's.' And its most common effect is to produce a kind of emotional withdrawal. The stepfather shuts the curtains, draws the blinds, and turns out the light on his stepkids. The rule has a corollary, though. Being able to give a biological child everything you feel he deserves in the way of time and affection usually makes a stepdad much more forthcoming with his stepkids. The curtains stay open and the light on.

"In terms of your stepfamily, Roger, this rule means the closer you stay to Max, the more open and relaxed you'll be with Noah and Donovan. So for everyone's sake, it's important that you and Max remain close. But how do you do that?

"With your new responsibilities, there'll be less time for long, leisurely weekends together and less time still for those two-week hiking trips to Nova Scotia every August. From now on, Ann will expect you to spend August on Martha's Vineyard with her and her family, which means, if you're going to continue seeing as much of Max as you do now, from now on that will have to happen within the context of your new stepfamily, and that means you'll have to make Max feel so comfortable in it that he'll want to come along when the Levines decamp to the Vineyard for August or to the Maine woods for a long Fourth of July weekend.

"One thing that makes a tremendous difference in a child's comfort index, Roger, is having a friend around. So one way you can make Max feel at home in your stepfamily is by encouraging a friendship between him and your stepkids. The age and sex differences make Donovan an unsuitable candidate, but Noah and Max are both boys and fairly close in age. So they start out with two natural affinities, which you can help to cement by suggesting things the three of you can do together, like taking in a baseball or basketball game."

"What about Donovan, Ron. Won't she feel left out?"

"If you're worried about that, by all means invite her along. But I doubt that she'll accept or that she'll feel hurt if the three of you go ahead without her. There aren't many certainties in this world, but one of them is that a teenage girl would rather do just about anything than spend an afternoon at a ballpark with three males, two of whom are under the age of ten.

"By the way, have you and Ann talked about where Max is going to stay yet?"

"Not yet, Ron."

"Do, then. Because having a place of his own at Dad's house can also add measurably to a child's comfort index. Ideally, this space should be a room of his own, but failing that, a private space in the den, family room, or his stepbrother's or -sister's room will do. What's important is that the space belong exclusively to him and that he be allowed to stake a territorial claim to it by keeping some of his clothes and toys there.

"Your stepkids' willingness to share will also have an important influence on Max's comfort index, Roger."

"Their toys and games?"

"Yes, those, but their house, too. You know how territorial kids can be. A new visitor sits in a chair and suddenly they want to sit in it; he puts on a TV program and they want to watch another one. If Noah and Donovan behave this way with Max, visiting your house will feel like sleeping on a bed of nails to him. At first he won't want to come, and eventually he'll refuse to come.

"You know the member of the firm we haven't talked about yet, Roger—you. What you want from the role will also determine what kind of a stepdad you become. And let me warn you—the human heart is an unpredictable thing. You may go into your relationship with Noah and Donovan thinking you want one thing from it, only to discover a year or two from now that you really want something entirely different."

This happens to stepdads all the time. Peter Cohen, one of the men who was in our stepfathering program a few years ago, had never felt much natural affinity for girls. So when he married his present wife, Joyce, three years ago, he more or less decided that he wanted to keep some distance between himself and Joyce's eleven-year-old, Tanya. "She's a nice enough kid," Pete told me a couple of weeks before the wedding, "but I don't see us getting close. She doesn't know who Larry Bird is and I don't know who the Cars are. Besides, my own son, Ben, pretty much fills me up as a dad."

Well, thirteen months later Peter was back in my office sitting where Roger was sitting, telling me all of the wonderful things he'd discovered in the meantime about girls in general and Tanya in particular. But then he went on to tell me she'd also become trapped by his initial decision to keep his distance. That had made him go into his relationship with Tanya with one arm up, and as he was discovering now, once a child thinks of you as having an arm up, it's very, very hard to make her think of you with two arms outstretched and open.

Allowing your initial preconceptions to shape your relationship with a stepchild is a trap a lot of stepdads fall into. And the best way to avoid it is to leave some room for your wants to change and grow. If you approach stepchildren with an "attitude" at first, you may find yourself trapped by that attitude if your feelings change later.

At the outset, the best policy for a stepdad to adopt is to be open and flexible toward his stepkids and self-aware. The first will keep you from being typecast the way Pete was by Tanya, and the second will give you the time and room you need to decide what kind of stepdad you want to become. For example, you may find your stepkids are so much fun, you want to get closer than you thought you would, or alternatively, you may find that it takes more energy than you want to spend to move that far in. Again, I don't know, but I do know that what you feel will help you answer these questions. So, for the first year or so, you should pay close attention to that voice of emotion inside you.

I told Roger that for the next two months it might even be a good idea to keep an emotional-response log. "A written record of your interactions with Noah and Donovan and the emotions they generate will reveal patterns that could help you decide whether you want to be the Big or Little Dipper in their particular Universe.

"Can I give you one last piece of advice, Rog? Don't feel guilty if you end up deciding you want to be the Little Dipper. It won't be a sign of failure. Every stepfather-stepchild relationship begins with several givens and these sometimes make a close relationship impossible—no matter what the stepfather wants.

"I've already mentioned the deep bond between the child and his biological father. There are many things you can be to a youngster with such a bond, but you can't be another father to him, and if you insist on that role and only that role, you'll rule out all the other roles you might play for him, like friend, adviser, big brother, or uncle.

"The second given is the stepchild's level of resistance. A certain amount—even a great deal—of stonewalling is normal in the first year or two. But there are kids—either because of personality peculiarities or feelings about their parents' divorce—who go on and on resisting. Should you find yourself stepparent to such a child, the best course is to bow to the inevitable—you and the child will never get close—and aim for a policy of peaceful coexistence.

"The third given is your personality and the way it interfaces with Noah's and Donovan's. You're an orderly man, Roger. You like things done on time, in sequence, and with all the details wrapped up. I don't know what your stepkids are like, but if they have the same kind of temperament, building a close relationship with them will be easy. But if they're more freewheeling than you, it will be harder, and if they're very freewheeling, it might be impossible.

"Human relationships are full of natural fits and misfits. And since there's nothing you can do about that, the only thing you can do with Noah and Donovan is hope for the best, and bow to the inevitable if you get second best. It's not your fault if the three of you aren't a natural fit, and it's not your stepkids' fault; it's just the way things are." I told Roger, the last member of the firm he needed to be aware of was the ghost of marriages past. It's made up of all the broken hopes and dreams and all the disappointments you and Ann are nursing from your first marriages. This ghost is the firm's bad guy. Not only can it undermine you with Noah and Donovan; it can also undermine you with Ann."

"How, Ron?"

"By playing on your expectations and fantasies. Couples like you and Ann are eager to make up for those failed first marriages, and so the ghost speaks in the siren song of instant happiness and gratification. 'You're right,' it'll tell you, 'this time it will be completely different. You're going to get everything you want: the ten-speeds in the front yard, the big maple in the back, and the happy family to put under it. And you're going to get them all right away.'

"Life isn't like that, Roger. I know it, you and Ann know it, and the ghost knows it. But it also knows that it's easy to forget what you know when you have visions of sugar plums dancing in your head. So at the beginning it'll promise a couple like you and Ann all the sugar plums you want: 'Would you like instant paternal authority, unity on every issue, and a big English sheep dog to go along with the ten-speeds, the maple, and the happy family?' Your every wish is the ghost's command because it knows the higher a couple's initial expectations, the quicker they'll be tempted to throw in the towel later when the inevitable fighting and friction develop.

"I don't know if you've seen the divorce rate on second marriages, Roger, but it's a tribute to the ghost's wiliness. It runs at between fifty and sixty percent or about one and one-half times the average for first marriages.

"The best way to deal with the ghost's sweet talk is to keep reminding Ann and yourself of this fact. Anytime a group of relative strangers comes together to live in the intimate circumstances of a nuclear family, one or two years of friction and fighting are inevitable before everyone settles in. This will keep your expectations and Ann's earthbound and your marriage safe.

"Roger, you look like you're bursting to ask a question."

"I am, Ron. What in God's name do I do during those one or two years while everyone's settling in?"

"Simple. You wake up every morning and say to yourself, 'Roger, today, let a smile be your umbrella.' "

11

Working Together

Into my office one fine June morning marched Sam Aberjanassi, who pulled up a chair next to my desk, sat down and said, "Boy, Ron, am I confused. Olympia graduates from law school this month and I want to be happy for her, I really do. But every time I start telling myself how hard she's worked for her law degree, and how wonderful it is that she's already been offered a terrific job, a little voice inside me starts whispering, 'Hold on a minute, pal. What's Ricky and Denisa's life going to be like without a stay-at-home mom? And what about you, Sam? Without Olympia at home, how will you get by?' "

Sam's little voice has been whispering in a lot of other male ears lately. And if the issues it raises always seem to be troubling ones, well, recent research shows that life in a dual-career family can be troubling. Out of resentment and insecurity some of its male members have been found to retreat into themselves; out of guilt and role overload some of its female members have been found to lose their maternal sensitivity. And out of a lack of parental support, some of its younger members have been found to suffer developmental setbacks.

Sam's little voice, however, isn't telling the entire story about life in a dual-career family. Another, happier group of studies shows that, under the right circumstances, life in such a family can have a transforming effect on its members. Women express more of their independent, competence-oriented sides, men more of their nurturing sides, and as this cross-fertilization grows and flourishes, the children in such families benefit. Following Mom's example, girls display more self-reliance and, following Dad's, boys show more emotional expressivity and openness.

For the Aberjanassis, as for millions of other dual-career families, the challenge, of course, is creating those "right circumstances." Studies show that *everyone* in a dual-career family flourishes when Mom and Dad feel that their professional and personal needs are understood, respected, and supported. And they also show that the best way to create an environment of mutual respect and support is through mutual commitment. The couple has to divide household and child-care chores in a way that leaves both feeling fairly treated.

Most husbands and wives assume this means a straightforward fifty-fifty division of labor. But the key to creating a workable and lasting agreement isn't percentages, but comfort of fit. No one will honor an agreement that doesn't also honor his—or her—background and upbringing. And of the three responsibility-sharing formulas available to dual-career couples the one that is most likely to ignore the background and upbringing of its cosigners is a straightforward fifty-fifty division of labor. Nothing in a man's background prepares him to be a complete coequal in the domestic sphere, and nothing in a woman's prepares her to live comfortably with the loss of maternal and domestic prerogatives such a division of labor would involve.

The second option available to dual-career families like the Aberjanassis has the advantage of honoring a man's background. But it has the more serious disadvantage of making his wife a candidate for role overload, since a traditional responsibility-sharing agreement brings the historical division of labor between the sexes (the woman does everything) into a dual-career family.

No one can shoulder the responsibilities involved in being a full-time worker, parent, cook, and maid. And when a woman tries, either because she has to or because she wants to, everyone suffers. She herself suffers because the strain of trying to be all things to all people eventually takes its toll on her physical and emotional health; her children suffer because the strain is associated with the kinds of maternal behaviors that can create developmental risks for a youngster in a dual-career family; and her husband suffers, too, because eventually the strain will take its toll on their marriage. If the woman isn't getting the help she wants and needs, she'll be angry and resentful, and even if she's doing it all out of choice, she'll be so exhausted by the effort that she won't have any energy left over for the intimacies that renew a marriage and keep it vibrant.

The third option available to dual-career couples, an equitable responsibility-sharing agreement, is based on the principle of fairness. It recognizes that for both practical and psychological reasons, a dual-career family can't function without an equitable division of household and child-care chores. But it also recognizes that the continuing pull of tradition and the individual differences between couples makes a fair division of labor a relative thing. What seems fair to a couple with one set of wants, needs, values, and resources will seem unfair to another couple with a different set.

I told Sam his family and the Cronins were good illustrations of this principle. "Before Maureen got pregnant," I said, "she had an undemanding job at the telephone company, two older kids, and very few outside commitments, so Paul's ten percent contribution made to the house and kids seemed very fair to her, and, of course, words can't describe how fair it seemed to Paul.

"You and Olympia, on the other hand, have two young children, she's about to enter a fast-track law career, and, if I recall, she's also pretty active in your community. So a ten percent contribution by you wouldn't seem fair to her or, probably, to you either, Sam. In fact, I suspect, in time you would begin feeling guilty about the bad case of role overload this level of help was giving Olympia, and the effect it was having on Ricky and Denisa. Have you thought about what she'd consider a fair contribution from you?"

Sam shook his head.

"Have you thought about what *you'd* consider a fair contribution from you?"

Sam shook his head again.

"These are the two questions you'll have to answer to achieve an equitable agreement, Sam. And let me tell you how to answer them in a way that may make everyone happy. First, define how much you'll be comfortable contributing; next, determine the maximum you'll be asked to contribute; then subtract the difference between the two and compromise between the two positions.

"The first step is important because in order to sustain

an equitable agreement, you not only have to be fair to Olympia; you must also be fair to yourself. Otherwise, everything will come unstuck. You'll stew and fume about the injustice of the agreement the two of you have made, until finally you blow up and bring it crashing down on everyone's head. So before you do anything else, you have to determine how much you'll be able to help Olympia and still feel fairly treated yourself. At the project we call this determination a man's *stretchability quotient* and there are two ways of determining it.

"One is by examining your upbringing. Often, when a man says, 'I'm being asked to do too much,' what he is really saying is 'I'm being asked to do something that makes me feel unmanly.' And since every man's ideas about masculinity are shaped by his father, whether or not your dad helped out around the house or with you will have a big effect on how large a stretch you'll be able to make comfortably for Olympia. How was your dad in these departments, Sam?"

"Average, Ron. He took care of the family finances, did minor repairs around the house, mowed the lawn, and, once in a while, if we had company, he'd help with the dishes later. I'd say he was a fairly typical man of his generation in his fathering, too. A lot of his nights were spent at the office working, but Saturdays and Sundays, he always found time for me and my sister, Maria. Overall, I'd say that while he helped, he wasn't overburdened domestically."

"Level of involvement doesn't matter, Sam. In terms of your stretchability quotient, the key is involvement itself. Your dad gave you a model and you can build on that. You'll find it easier to pick up a dish or broom and feel manly because you saw him do these things and still feel manly. The men who have the narrowest stretchability quotients are the ones who didn't have dads like yours. Because they spent their childhoods watching their fathers watch their mothers do everything, they feel it's unfair for a wife to ask them to do anything."

Dave Pullio was like this. Dave grew up in one of those traditional homes where any display of domesticity was considered the kiss of death to a man. So when his wife, Rose, got a job at the Motor Vehicles Department last December, Dave was beside himself. Every time she asked him to pick up a dish he felt as if he were being asked to put on a dress.

When Dave asked me what to do, I told him he had three options. He could do nothing—which would not only be unfair to Rose but would alienate her. He could seek professional help to work out his conflicts—you can imagine how happy that suggestion made Dave. Or he could use one of his friends as a model of male involvement. Fortunately, Dave had such a friend, one of his buddies at the Knights of Columbus, Tony LoPresto.

Tony's background is similar to Dave's. But Tony is also one of those men who love to cook. So when his wife went back to work a few years ago, Tony found it relatively easy to step in and pick up the slack, because it gave him a chance to do more of something he liked—cooking. I told Dave to talk to Tony, which he did, and the reassurance and advice Tony passed on turned out to be very helpful. Bit by bit, Dave's building his stretchability quotient. In fact, at Dominick's graduation party, Rose told me she thinks by this time next year Dave will probably even be willing to wear an apron when he washes the dishes.

"The second factor that determines a man's stretchability quotient, Sam, is his own experience as a husband and father. A man who's always helped out domestically has some history and knowledge to draw on, and this gives him a bigger margin for a comfortable stretch when his wife goes back to work. But a man who's never done anything feels like he's just landed on Mars. Everything around him suddenly looks cold, hostile, and a little threatening.

"With Olympia in law school for the last few years, you must have been pretty involved around the house and with Ricky and Denisa."

"Very involved, Ron. I make dinner for the kids the two nights a week Olympia has evening classes. I do the weekly grocery shopping and all the yard chores, and most of the time I pick up the cleaning and drop off Ricky at school. That's a lot. Do you think I can stretch any more than I already have?"

I told Sam I thought he could.

"Given your high stretchability quotient, I think you could comfortably push up what sounds like a fifteen percent contribution to a twenty-five, thirty—who knows, maybe a thirty-five percent contribution. The problem is I think Olympia will ask for even more, Sam. But we won't know how much more until we've finished the next step in an equitable responsibility-sharing formula, which is to calculate how much you'll be asked to contribute."

The best way to compute this request is to look at the factors a woman looks at when she's considering how much help to ask for. One of the most important is the nature of her work. Is it time-consuming? Is it emotionally and/ or intellectually demanding? The more likely a woman is to answer yes to each of these questions, the more likely she is to ask for a large time contribution.

"And you think Olympia will answer yes to all of them?" Sam asked.

"A fast-track law career is pretty demanding, Sam."

The recent research on maternal employment is another factor that often weighs heavily in women's requests for help. These data show that while working mothers tend to have more problems with their children, they do so not because they work but because they don't get help needed to be both a full-time mother and a worker. So when a woman sees studies like a recent University of Michigan one, which shows that working mothers display fewer positive behaviors toward their youngsters, and a recent University of Utah one, which shows that they also sometimes become less sensitive to their children's needs, a woman thinks: "The way for me to avoid these hazards is to get more help from my husband."

"I'm sure Olympia's seen these or similar studies, Sam," I said. "The research on maternal employment's been pretty widely publicized."

"Olympia reads a lot, Ron."

Knowing how the Aberjanassis had historically divided household chores, I thought a sense of entitlement also might have an important influence on Olympia's thinking. For the past ten years, she'd been covering almost all of the family's domestic bases, leaving Sam free to pursue his career goals. Wives who do this often feel entitled to a big quid pro quo when their turn comes.

"How big a quid pro quo?" a worried-looking Sam asked.

"Big, Sam. I think Olympia will tell you a forty-five—fifty-five split—fifty-five for her, forty-five for you—would let her handle the demands of her job, avoid the hazards that the job can pose to her mothering, and give you a chance to pay back the debt she feels she's owed."

Sam looked very worried now.

"I may have a large stretchability quotient, but I can't stretch all the way up to forty-five percent. Even you agree on that."

I told Sam that Step Three of the formula would deliver him from the dilemma Steps One and Two had put him in. It's premised on the belief that the first two steps will often identify large discrepancies between what a wife wants and what a husband can give, and on the further belief that out of love and goodwill a couple will be willing to resolve these discrepancies through negotiation. One gives a bit on the laundry, the other on the school pickup, until, finally, they've achieved the goal of Step Three: a compromise between their respective positions that leaves both feeling fairly treated.

You can get a pretty good idea of how this goal is achieved from the negotiation role play Sam and I did during his visit. It started with a question from me. "Sam," I asked, "what forty-five percent of the household and child-care chores do you think Olympia will ask you to take over?"

"I'll be asked to take charge of the breakfast and dinner shifts, to do the bills, which takes three or four hours every other week, and to drop off Denisa at day care and Ricky at school. Olympia will also want me to help out with the children's visits to the doctor and dentist."

"What would you consider a fair counterproposal?" I asked

"I'm prepared to do all I'm already doing plus the dishes every night and the bills every other Saturday. I want you to know that's a big sacrifice for me, Ron. Saturday's my golf day."

"I know. And I'm sure Olympia will appreciate your sacrifice. What else would you offer in your counterproposal?"

Sam looked at me crossly.

"You're only up to between twenty and twenty-two percent, Sam. You've still got plenty of room to stretch."

"All right, Ron. I'll also take responsibility for some of the doctor and dentist visits. But that's it. I can't do any more."

Frank Deveraux, another former program dad, had said the same thing to me a few years ago when he dropped by to complain about his wife, Doris's, request for some extra evening help. Doris had just gotten a probationary promotion to group manager at her bank and during the trial period she felt she'd need the flexibility to work late some nights. I told Sam that Frank understood, even sympathized with his wife's concerns. But he also felt he was already doing enough. So when Doris asked about the extra help he told her, "Look, if you're worried about your nights, get a woman in to make dinner for the kids and put them to bed."

"That sounds like a reasonable solution to me," Sam said.

"Frank thought so, too, Sam. But Doris couldn't find a woman willing to come in nights and, without that extra support, she lost the promotion. About four months into her probation she was told things weren't working out, and that so depressed her, she began to withdraw. It was over a year before she was herself again, and, in that interval, just to keep his family and marriage afloat, Frank had to increase his contribution by four hundred percent."

I pointed out to Sam that taking Ricky and Denisa four nights would sizably decrease Olympia's chances of ending up like Doris Deveraux and his of ending up like Frank.

"Bend a little now, so I won't have to bend more later, Ron."

"Exactly, Sam. Now, would you like to see the chores you've committed yourself to?" I said, handing Sam the piece of paper where I'd listed those commitments. The list read:

- Be responsible for Ricky and Denisa's dinners, baths, and bedtimes four nights a week.
- Do the family bills every other Saturday.
- Do the weekly shopping.
- Be in charge of all cleaning drop-offs and pickups.
- Oversee the kids' doctor and dentist visits.

Sam reminded me that he'd only agreed to take responsibility for some of the visits to the doctor and dentist.

"That's true," I said. "But your status as the family's veteran employee makes you the logical candidate to shoulder all responsibilities in this area. No one minds when a trusted veteran employee asks for an occasional morning or afternoon off. But they do mind when a new employee does."

"I hadn't thought about that, Ron."

I asked Sam whether my list was acceptable to him.

"Yes."

"Congratulations," I said, "you and Olympia have now achieved the goal of an equitable compromise between your two positions. Olympia will get all the help and support she needs—if not everything she might ask for—and you'll only have to push your contribution up from fifteen to thirty percent, which still leaves you well within your stretchability quotient."

I told Sam I foresaw only one potential problem.

"Olympia won't like the agreement, Ron?"

"No, Sam," I said. "I think she'll be pleased by it; very pleased, in fact. The problem, if there is one, will be getting her to stick to it. Most of the things that make it hard for a man to give domestically make it hard for a woman to give up domestically. Olympia spent her childhood watching her mother take care of her and her brothers and sisters, prepare the meals, do the cleaning, look after her father, and most of her adult life has been spent doing these things for her own family. And that creates its own kind of stretchability quotient.

"No matter how demanding or rewarding her professional life, there'll always be a side of Olympia that whispers, 'Are you doing enough as a mother and a wife?' And in time, if this voice is loud and insistent enough, it can also lead Olympia down the path to role overload. She'll tell you she's happy to accept your help, but five months from now, you'll suddenly find her getting up at five every morning to precook a meat loaf or roast for dinner, and to iron the kids' clothes.

"These days, there are a lot of women who want to be Betty Crocker, Mister Rogers, and Lee Iacocca wrapped into one. And if Olympia should turn out to be one of them, you'll be tempted to let her try because it will make your life easier."

Sam looked puzzled. "I should insist she let me live up to my side of the agreement?"

"What you should do if this happens, Sam, is listen carefully. There are few individuals of either sex who are talented or energetic enough to be superstars in every sphere of life, and the strain of trying can produce severe stress. So if Olympia should set her sights on becoming a superwoman, one other thing you should do is be on the alert for the kinds of hidden thoughts and feelings that signal the presence of role overload.

"You rememer Bill Gates, don't you, Sam? I saw the two of you talking at our Christmas party. His wife, Francesca, fell into the superwoman trap. Francesca's a lovely woman, Sam, but very perfectionistic and demanding, especially about herself. So, a few years ago, when Bill told me she'd taken a programming job with one of the computer companies on Route 128, I warned him to be on the alert—Francesca's personality made her a perfect candidate for the syndrome."

"And, Ron?"

"And Francesca threw herself into the job the way she throws herself into everything else, body and soul, which might have been all right if she hadn't also insisted on maintaining her primacy in the house and with the kids. Bill had offered to help; in fact, he'd made a very generous offer. But Francesca said she didn't need it. And for the first six months or so, it seemed she didn't. But then, out of the blue, she began complaining about the people at work, about their friends, about the other parents on her PTA committee. Bill knew what such out-of-character behavior signaled, and so one night when Francesca complained that she couldn't get a decision out of her boss, Bill picked up on it."

"You need him to give you a yes or no by Monday and time is running short?" Bill asked.

"Very short," Francesca said. "I don't know what I'm going to do if I can't get an answer out of him."

"You really feel pressured," Bill said, reflecting back the unstated message in her statement.

"I always feel pressured," she said. "Bill, maybe I'm doing too much."

"And there it was. In the midst of a simple conversation, Francesca's guard suddenly slipped and out popped an admission she'd been resisting for months. She and Bill had a long conversation that night—longer than they'd had since either could remember when. And by the end of it, Francesca had agreed to stop trying to do everything and to accept Bill's help."

As I finished, I noticed that Sam was looking at his watch.

"I know, Sam," I said, "I've got to run, too. I've got a class in ten minutes. But before we go, let me give you a final piece of advice. If the day should come when you find Olympia making as much or even more money than you, don't let that become an issue between the two of you. Your marriage is too important to be put at risk by professional competition. Besides, Olympia's contribution will allow you to relax and begin enjoying your kids and your life a little more."

"Okay. Anything else, Ron?"

"Just good luck, Sam. I think you and Olympia are going to do fine."